Lowercase

HAYLEY B HALLIWELL

Copyright © 2025 by Hayley B Halliwell

Cover Art Copyright © 2025 by Ali Shearer

All rights reserved.

No part of this book may be reproduced in any form or by any electronic or mechanical means, including information storage and retrieval systems, without written permission from the author, except for the use of brief quotations in a book review.

No part of this book may be used to train generative AI technologies.

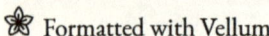 Formatted with Vellum

For Shanna. For Mom.
For anyone who knows the power of grief and survivor's guilt.
For 7-year-old me, who always said she'd have a novel on the shelves one day.

Contents

Chapter 1	1
Chapter 2	15
Chapter 3	25
Chapter 4	34
Chapter 5	53
Chapter 6	63
Chapter 7	77
Chapter 8	91
Chapter 9	105
Chapter 10	121
Chapter 11	133
Chapter 12	148
Chapter 13	163
Chapter 14	175
Chapter 15	189
Chapter 16	204
Chapter 17	219
Chapter 18	235
Chapter 19	247
Chapter 20	258
Chapter 21	271
Chapter 22	286
Acknowledgments	297
About the Author	301
About the Cover Artist	303
Also by Hayley B Halliwell	305

One

Mom smiles and gives an almost imperceptible nod as the waitress passes our table again. "So, what's the plan, Little Elle?" she asks, shaking her auburn hair out of the way before taking another bite off her fork.

I swallow my food, not much thought going into my answer when we've had this planned out for years. "Well, we start by sending Oakvale a notification of our acceptance."

"Look at you with your big words, ready for college or something." Lilah, my best friend since forever and the closest thing to a sister I've ever known, nudges me with her elbow. Even with my red hair and green eyes to her brown hair and eyes, we often do get mistaken for being sisters.

One corner of Mom's mouth turns up. "After that, I mean. The big plan."

I take a deep breath and set my fork down so I can count the list off on my fingers. "Go to college, live in dorms the first year–"

"Full college experience." Lilah makes air quotes as she says it, poking fun at my need for all the experiences we can fit into one life. She makes fun, but she wants the adventure as much as I do.

"Oakvale makes all students live in dorms the first year, you know this," I remind her, knowing very well that she hasn't forgotten.

"Doesn't mean I have to be happy about it." She rolls her eyes a little too dramatically, taking a bite of her food in much the same fashion.

"I think you'll survive it for one year," Mom says, clearly amused at our exchange.

"Ah-*em*." I clear my throat, adding to the drama, and continue counting the list off on my fingers. "After that, we just need to study hard, make the Dean's list, work part-time around classes, graduate–"

"From our number one college." Lilah taps her fork against the fingers I'm counting. Thankfully, it wasn't still covered in food. You never know with her.

"Yes, and then move back home and get really good jobs with our new degrees." I run the list through my head one more time to make sure I'm not leaving anything major off. Like I said, Lilah and I have been planning this for years, down to every schedule-able detail. We're only doing this once and I don't want to miss any of the experiences we're supposed to have.

Or worse, choose the wrong ones.

Mom smiles, her pride clear. "That sounds like a grown up plan to me."

"You hear that, Ellessy? We're grown ups now. We should have ordered wine." Lilah raises her glass of soda.

Mom snorts. "Don't get ahead of yourself, kid."

"It was worth a try." Lilah shrugs, but doesn't hide her smirk.

The waitress comes back and asks how we're doing right as we all have food in our mouths, of course. She smiles and moves on, not making the awkward moment last longer than necessary.

"You forgot to work in time to find a strong, sexy brainiac to fall in love with and make my degree useless." Lilah's mischievous grin makes it hard to tell how much of that is a joke.

"Do I need to worry about you corrupting my daughter?" Knowing Mom, she's mostly joking and only a little serious.

"It's a little late for that." Lilah elbows me again and snickers.

"Can I eat without being violated, please?" I elbow her back.

"Don't make me change my mind about paying for your dinner. Both of you." Mom smiles, but the arch in her brow says enough.

She worries about me, about both of us. Lilah has been like her bonus daughter since kindergarten. And I know she's hiding a lot more anxiety than she's letting on about us leaving.

Mom has a rough past. I know she's worried we'll make mistakes like she did.

We're not going to do that, though. We're going to follow the plan and live the dream for real and be able to give her a better life on top of it.

"You don't need to worry, anyway, Mom. Falling in love is not in the plan until after college." They both snort, as if on cue. I look from one to the other. "What? There won't be time!"

I know I sound naïve, but there really won't be time. Not with classes and clubs and school related activities on top of working and hanging out with friends in what little spare time is left.

What kind of relationship would that be? Not one

I'm interested in. Not one I need. And definitely not one that is in the plans.

"Oh my Little Elle," Mom brushes a strand of hair behind my ear and gives my chin a squeeze. "Love isn't something you can work your plans around. It just happens. Whether you want it to or not."

"And I plan to fall in love at least twice." Lilah watches a guy walk past our table and nods, repeating herself, "At least twice."

"Does your mother know where your hormones are at?" Mom asks.

"She says that's why she's thankful I have your daughter to keep me on the right path."

Mom smiles, but I catch the pain hiding behind it. "Just don't do what I did." She could have easily said not to fall in love with someone who is hiding a drug addiction, but she doesn't need to. We've heard what she went through with my father.

I reach forward and squeeze her hand. "Not a chance."

Lilah places her hand over ours. "You taught us how to catch a snake, Mama Porter."

"We know what to watch out for, Mom, don't worry."

"Yeah, and I'll cut his head off before he can hurt

either one of us, anyway." Lilah takes her hand back and slides a finger across her neck, snapping them at the end.

Mom fights a grin. "Glad to know you girls listen to me on occasion."

"Only on occasion," I say, winking at her.

Mom scoffs as our waitress stops by, setting fresh drinks on our table.

"That goes for life, too, you know," Lilah says. She shoves a mouthful of food into her mouth.

"What does?" I ask, picking my fork back up for another bite.

She talks as she chews her own food. "Not being able to plan around love and it just happening or whatever. I'm pretty sure life works that way, too."

"You plan what you can and leave wiggle room for the rest of it," Mom says.

I shake my head and swallow. "I like having a plan. It keeps things from going wrong. And if that plan doesn't have room for a relationship right now–which it doesn't–then it's not happening." I laugh and make a face at both of them to settle my point.

Having control means things don't go wrong. Making a plan gives me control.

Mom and Lilah share a look. "I will leave all of the

plans in your capable hands, Elle. Even if they're not fun." Lilah picks up a dessert menu and adds, "And if there's no plans for love, then I'll start working on that 'Freshman Fifteen' instead."

"You haven't even finished the food you have now." I point my fork at the few bites left on her plate. The only thing Lilah ever plans for is her next snack. I'd be lying if I said I didn't love that about her.

"So? I thought we were celebrating?" Her eyes light up as she flips through the pages.

Mom plucks the dessert menu out of Lilah's hands. "We can grab something on the way home."

"Have I mentioned lately that you never have to tell me twice when it comes to food?"

"Yes, Lilah." Literally, before we left the house for the restaurant.

The waitress pops by again, eyeing the dessert menu in Mom's hand, and asks if we want anything else.

"No, thank you." Mom sets the menu back where it was.

"I'll just leave this here for you then." She places the bill on the table and leaves. Mom tucks enough cash into the folder to cover dinner and a nice tip. She really spent too much on us, but I know that's why we're getting dessert on the way home. Goodwin's Steakhouse isn't too expensive, but it's pricey enough that we save it for special occasions.

Mom places the folder with the money and her empty plate in the center of the table. "You girls just about ready, then?"

"I was ready the moment you said we could get dessert," Lilah says as we add our plates to the stack.

"Alright, then let's get moving before traffic beats us to it." Mom takes one last drink from her glass before scooting out of the booth to leave.

"Is it cool with you if Lilah stays tonight?" I ask as we're walking out.

"I already figured she was going to."

"I really should have my own room at this point, Ms. Porter," Lilah says.

"I'd offer you the guest room, but we both know you wouldn't use it."

"Not when bunk beds are the better option."

"Are you going to pay for them?" Mom arches her brow.

Lilah doesn't miss a beat. "That's what the degree is for."

I love when they banter like this. When I say Lilah is Mom's "bonus daughter", I really mean it. Her parents aren't bad people, but they work a lot. Lilah is an only child and I think she spent more time at our house than her own growing up.

I don't want to say Mom raised her, but it wouldn't be unfair to say, either.

We squeeze through the busy lobby and hurry out to Mom's car, Lilah ahead of me. "I've got front this time." I say. "You had it on the way here, remember?"

She throws her head back and groans, stopping in front of the passenger side door. "Fine. But I'm sitting behind Mama Porter, then. I know how gassy you get when we eat here, and I'm not about to be right behind that." She plugs her nose and points at me.

"Ha. Ha," I say, deadpan, pushing her aside. "Very funny." I can tell she's only partly teasing.

"Hey, you know how you get."

"You both better hold your gas if you want dessert," Mom says. "Now get in and buckle up."

There isn't much traffic on the road at first, but it doesn't take long before more cars start pouring onto the road with us.

"It might be a few minutes before we get there at this rate, girls." Mom adjusts her mirror.

"Gives us time to work off dinner." Lilah says. I turn back to see her slapping her tummy.

"Work it off how? You're not even moving," I say.

"How great would that be, though? If we could just work off weight by going on car rides?" We both burst into giggles at the idea.

Mom shakes her head, laughing quietly to herself. "I still can't believe you girls are heading off to college in a few months. How did you grow up so fast?"

"Genetics, probably," Lilah says.

"The natural plan of life?" I offer.

"It only took one sentence from each of you to remind me it's about time you moved out."

Lilah leans forward, resting her chin on her hand between us. "You know we'll be back to bug you on the weekends."

"Like darling little roaches." Mom glances down at her, quick to put her eyes back on the road. "Now, sit back like you're supposed to."

Lilah settles back in the seat and asks, "Don't roaches survive until the end of the world?" I turn to look back at her again as she continues, "Picture it: Lilah Day. Lina and Ellessy Porter. Last roaches left on Earth."

Mom snorts. "Sounds like a bad movie."

"But we'd be stars, Mama Porter." Lilah stretches her arms like she's making a rainbow in front of her.

"Wouldn't there be other roaches if they all survive?" I ask, raising a brow.

She drops her hands to her lap. "Fine. Best roaches left on Earth. Same difference."

I cringe at the phrase. "That doesn't make sense. There's no such thing as a 'same difference'."

"Sure there is, if you believe hard enough." She flashes me a cheeky grin, wiggling her head with it.

"The peace and quiet I'll have when you girls leave is going to be a shock."

"You'll miss us," Lilah says.

"Of course I will." Mom glances at her in the rearview mirror and then to me. "And then I'll miss the peace and quiet as soon as you're back."

"Gee thanks, Mom." She's the only person I know with quick enough wit to match Lilah's.

"That's just mean, Ms. Porter." Lilah feigns offense.

"Oh, you know I love you girls." Mom reaches over and squeezes my knee.

"Yeah, yeah. We love you, too." Lilah pokes her tongue out but Mom's eyes are on the road.

It's weird to think this isn't going to be our normal anymore. Not like this, anyway. This time tomorrow we'll be accepting admission at Oakvale University and getting ready to start worrying about class schedules and majors and dorm rooms and jobs that work with all that.

I turn back to Lilah again. "Hey, whe–"

I struggle to open my eyes through the heaviness keeping them closed. A dull ache radiates through my body with a dark feeling I can't shake.

"Ellessy?" I turn toward the voice, wincing at the sudden pain in my neck. A woman leans over me.

"Where am I?" A hoarse whisper of a voice escapes my lips.

She speaks slowly, like she's giving me extra time to process her words. "Ellessy, my name is Anna. I'm a nurse at Rook County Medical Center. You were in a car accident, okay?"

I glance around, the blue and white of the room making it clear this isn't home. The woman checks something on a monitor next to my bed. There are bags hanging next to it, dripping liquid into tubes that lead to an IV in my arm.

Fear surges through me, freezing me in place.

This isn't right.

"What happened?" The words rush out of my mouth.

"How is your pain, Ellessy? Can you give me a

number on a scale of zero to ten, zero being no pain and ten being the worst pain you've ever felt?"

That dark feeling grows when she doesn't answer my question. I mumble a "six" as I try to find the last thing I remember. What am I doing here?

I jerk forward, panic rising in my chest. "Where's Mom? Where's Lilah?" The last thing I remember is the three of us leaving the restaurant. Foggy, soundless images of us getting into the car and pulling away fade in and out. Nothing after that. Not even a hint of how I ended up here or the car accident this nurse mentioned.

Something deep in me whispers that I'm about to hear something I don't want to hear.

The nurse looks into my eyes as if she's searching for something. Finally, she says, "Ellessy, this was a very bad accident. You've sustained a lot of injuries–"

I cut her off, the words rushing out. "Lilah's dead, isn't she?" Something in me knows. I don't know how, but I just know. I can feel it like an empty space in my chest.

She frowns, slowly shaking her head. "Your friend did not survive."

I don't let myself grieve yet. I can't.

My voice cracks even more, tears streaming down my face as I ask, "And Mom?"

"Your mother is here in the hospital. She's... she's in a coma."

I close my eyes and give in, crying massive, ugly sobs that sound even worse with my voice as it is.

Lilah's gone.

Mom's in a coma.

Why am I okay?

Two

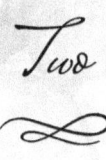

It feels like hours before the tears run dry. Maybe it is, I don't know. Time doesn't feel the same anymore.

A man walks into my room, hands tucked into the pockets on the front of his white coat. The nurse from before follows behind him. "I'm Dr. Forsyth." He pauses a moment, studying me. "Can you tell me what your name is?"

I want so much to yell at him that my name doesn't matter, that I don't matter, that the only thing that matters is making sure no one else dies while I'm still alive. "Ellessy Porter."

"Can you give me your middle name, too?"

"Jane."

He nods. "And your birthday?"

"March 19th." This feels like an interview.

"Good. And can you tell me how old you are?"

"Eighteen." The same age as Lilah.

Dr. Forsyth rubs his hand across the bottom of his chin. "Miss Porter, can you tell me who this is?" He gestures to the nurse.

Why is he asking me this? "My nurse. I can't remember her name... something with an 'A' I think."

He nods again. "Anna."

"Yeah, Anna. Sorry." I'm usually good with names.

Dr. Forsyth says something to her. She starts taking notes on a clipboard as he continues. "And you remember speaking with her earlier this afternoon?" My gut tries to connect dots my mind hasn't found yet. I nod. "Good. Good, Miss Porter. It seems your short-term memory is making a comeback." He smiles.

That dark feeling comes back again as things start making sense. My short-term memory is making a comeback? "How long have I been here?" I ask, dread joining my party of emotions.

"You were brought in roughly seventy-two hours ago." Three days? I've lost that much time? "You sustained some serious injuries, Miss Porter. You spent the first 24 hours with us in a medically induced coma. Your memory has only lasted about fifteen minutes up until this afternoon."

I look at Anna and things fall into place. That feeling in my gut. Knowing I didn't want to hear what she had to say.

She's been telling me the same things, answering my same questions about Lilah and Mom, over and over for two days.

I've been experiencing this nightmare repeatedly since I got here.

"It's been three hours now, Dr. Forsyth," Anna says.

"We obviously can't know for sure, but this is a good sign that the worst of your short-term memory troubles are behind us. However, with any traumatic brain injury, short-term memory problems continuing to occur down the road isn't uncommon."

My stomach drops. A traumatic brain injury. Short-term memory problems continuing. On top of everything else I've been told... What more could be thrown at me?

He continues. "Miss Porter, the impact of the semi-trailer with your mother's vehicle caused damage to your brain on impact, and further damage resulting from your brain hitting the front and back of your skull."

"The traumatic brain injury," I say.

"Yes," Dr Forsyth confirms as he looks at Anna.

She checks my monitors and nods to him. He continues, "Outside of the TBI, you've got a lot of internal bruising, including your lungs."

"Is that why my voice is like this?" I gesture to my throat, as if to point to my hoarse voice that's barely there.

Anna answers my question this time. "You were intubated–uh, you had a tube inserted down your throat so you could breathe–when you were brought in, and you were placed in a medically induced coma. It's normal to experience some dryness, sore throat, and difficulty speaking."

I stroke my neck, thinking of the tube that had been in there, uncomfortable at the idea.

I swallow and take a deep breath, preparing myself. "What else?" I can tell there's something they're holding back.

Is my voice going to stay like this? Will my brain injury get worse? What is it?

Dr. Forsyth smiles, a tight smile that seems more like an automated reaction he's done a million times. "Surprisingly, you have no broken bones. You did have a laceration at the back of your head that we've closed with staples." I immediately feel for the spot and count six little rectangles as he goes on, "Miss Porter, sometimes with brain injuries, there can be paralysis. We ran some tests with you and found that you do, indeed, have partial paralysis in the left side of your body. Imaging showed no signs of damage to the spinal cord, so we believe it to be temporary. Nothing a little physical therapy can't help."

Paralysis.

His words sink in and I snatch the covers off my legs. My right leg moves. My left stays put. I scoot back on my hospital bed and a heaviness drags where my leg is.

How could I not even know?

I want to scream. I want to yell at everyone in the room, as if any of this might be their fault and yelling might fix the problem.

"We're happy with the improvement we've seen in you today, Miss Porter. We'd like to keep you in our care for a few more days at the very least, but I'm confident we can have you home sooner than previously expected."

A sudden realization hits me and I want to be sick. "Did I miss Lilah's funeral?"

Anna steps forward. "Her parents told me they were holding the visitation and funeral on Friday. That's the furthest they could push the date in hopes you could attend. They also asked me to tell you that you're in their prayers."

I close my eyes and take a deep breath. I haven't missed it. Lilah's parents thought of me...

Oh, Lilah's parents...

How hard it must have been for them to stop and see me surviving when their daughter didn't.

I shake my head and look at Dr. Forsyth and Anna again. "What is today?"

Anna hesitates. "Tuesday."

Alarm courses through me. "I can't miss it, she was practically my sister. I have to be there." I look down at my useless leg, begging it to work again, to let me leap from this bed and run to her.

"If we continue to see improvement between now and Friday morning," Dr. Forsyth says, pulling my attention back. "I'm willing to sign your release. Under conditions."

Adrenaline has me clinging to the hope his words give me. "What conditions?"

"You'll need someone there to assist you."

My heart sinks, the adrenaline quickly sinking away. "I don't have anyone." I have Mom and Lilah. No other close friends, no other family that I really know.

He raises a brow. "No one in your family can come stay with you?"

"My father died before I was born. All I have is my

mom and Li–" My voice catches in my throat. "I don't–I don't have anyone else." That was always fine before... I never thought it would be a problem.

"No aunts or uncles or cousins?" Anna asks, the hope I lost seeming to be in her voice now. "It doesn't have to be someone you're close to."

I have to be able to go to the funeral. I have to do something.

Even if that means doing something Mom would hate.

I clear the emotion from my throat and speak very carefully, the guilt already nagging at me. "My father had a sister. I don't know if she's still alive, or if she even knows who I am. But I–I guess she's all I've got." I can barely look him in the eyes. Mom is going to be furious.

Doctor Forsyth stares at me for a moment, biting his cheek and toying with a pen in his white coat's pocket. "Do you know her name?"

"Dylan Isaac. I don't know if she's gotten married or anything, though, so that might not be her name anymore."

"We'll see what we can find out." He says something I can't quite hear to Anna, and smiles at me one more time before leaving the room.

There's a part of me that hopes he can't find

anything and I'll have no reason to feel guilty for mentioning her and no reason for Mom to be mad.

But I can't miss Lilah's... Lilah's funeral. I can't miss it.

Anna pulls a wheelchair from the corner of the room and brings it to rest in front of me. "Are you ready to go see your mom?"

The tears threaten to well up in my eyes. Do I even deserve to see her?

I nod.

Anna moves the IV bags and other things hanging next to my monitor over to the hook on the wheelchair. She places a board on my bed and helps me scoot across it to get seated. I can't help but feel ashamed at how useless I am to myself right now.

I'm going through so many emotions right now, though, that shame feels right at home.

Anna kneels down in front of me, her voice soft as she speaks. "I want you to be prepared when we go over there, okay?"

A chill runs down my spine. What am I about to see? Why do I need to be prepared? I nod, not knowing how else to respond.

"Your mom has a breathing tube and a central line in her neck, kind of like your IV. She has a lot of bruising, and swelling, and there are some stitches on her face." She pauses before adding, "I don't want you to feel like you can't speak with her or touch her."

"Will she know?" I ask.

"I've had patients who remembered some of the things their loved ones said to them. Some even said that's what pushed them to keep fighting."

I can do that. I can let her know I'm here and help her push.

I have to. I can't lose her, too.

I take a deep breath and nod, letting her know I'm ready.

We go to another room that's similar to mine. Mom is lying in the bed, more tubes connected to her than what I woke up with. I don't look at her face, though. I can't bring myself to see that it's really her just yet.

Anna pushes me over to the bed, but I keep my eyes down. "I'll be right here, okay?" She gestures to the corner by the door. "Pretend it's just you and her."

I wait for Anna to walk away before I turn back to Mom, working up the strength to really look at her. There's a tube down her throat, connected to a machine that's breathing for her. Her face is so swollen, with two rows of stitches above her brow and across her chin. If it weren't for the box perm hair, I wouldn't even know this is Mom.

There's no expression on her face. No smile, no sign of the hard life she's lived at the corners of her eyes and mouth.

This isn't how it's supposed to be.

This isn't part of the plan.

Emotion catches up to me and the words sputter out of my mouth. "I'm sorry, Mom." Tears well up with the sob that catches in my throat. "I love you so much, and I'm so, so sorry... I'm sorry... I'm sorry..."

I bury my face in her side and cry like no one is watching, the guilt and anguish taking over.

Three

Dr. Forsyth didn't give too many details, but he was able to contact my aunt and she agreed to be my temporary caregiver. Just until Mom wakes up and can come back home. Or until I'm well enough to not need a caregiver, if that comes first.

I'm hoping for the second option.

It feels weird calling her my aunt. The only thing I really know about her other than that Mom hates her, is her name, Dylan. She's been here a little more than an hour, but we haven't had a chance to talk. She and Dr. Forsyth have been going over paperwork and everything for my discharge today.

One glance at the clock has me biting my cheek. Lilah's... her funeral is in an hour.

Her funeral.

Just the thought makes my head spin.

Anna enters the room with a bag that says "Rook County Hospital Gift Shop" across the front. "Your aunt asked me to bring this up to you." She opens it and pulls out a grey t-shirt and a pair of black leggings. "She thought you might appreciate this more than what you've got on now."

I look down at what I'm wearing. My clothes were cut off after the accident, so the hospital offered a baggy sweatshirt and sweatpants they keep for patients in this situation. They're not very comfortable and I'm sure I stand out even more than the wheelchair already makes me.

"Thank you," I tell her. I don't know what else to say.

"Oh, don't thank me, I only told her the right size." Anna pulls the curtain around and helps me change. I'm a child who can't put on her own pants. That will be one of the first things I work on. "There. That's better, right?" She pushes the curtain back to the wall.

"Sure." I glance at the clock again.

"They just had a few things left to go over, so it shouldn't be much longer." She pauses and adds, "You're not going to miss it, Elle, I promise."

My eyes meet hers and I feel the emotion threatening to bubble up, but Dr. Forsyth and Dylan return before it can get to me.

"I think that's everything, then," Dr. Forsyth says, eyes on me. "You've truly proven yourself determined with the progress you made to see your discharge today. I have no doubt that physical therapy will be much the same." How close was I to having to stay longer?

He hands a folder to Dylan. "This everything?" she asks. The slight twang in her deeper voice stands out the most.

"Yes, that should be." He turns back to me and adds, "Which means you're cleared to leave, Miss. Porter."

Anna helps me into my wheelchair and hands me a clear bag with my purse and house keys inside. "Your first appointment with physical therapy is on Monday. It's all in the paperwork."

"Okay."

She lingers a second longer before wishing me well and leaving with Dr. Forsyth.

Dylan steps through the tension she hardly seems to notice. "I know we're pushin' for time, so what say we skip the awkward stuff for now and get going?"

I glance at the clock again. If we leave now, we might just make it in time.

I nod and she moves behind my wheelchair.

The ride to the funeral is silent other than Dylan's GPS telling her where to go. I stare out the window, the tension in my body rising as we get closer to the funeral home.

Those words sound wrong in my head. We should be going to college and visiting dorms, not funeral homes and cemeteries.

The GPS tells us we're there and Dylan finds the closest space available to park. She hops out of her SUV and meets me at my door with the wheelchair. Using my right leg and Dylan's help, I get out of the front seat and settled into the chair.

Another thing I'll have to get used to.

Dylan pushes me up to the funeral home and my stomach drops further with every step. Someone opens the doors for us, but I don't catch who. All my focus is on holding it together, something I don't think I'll be able to do for long.

Dylan pushes me to the main room. People are still standing around and talking quietly, as if there isn't a casket sitting at the end of the room, as if Lilah's lifeless body isn't lying inside it.

A cold sweat hits me as we keep moving forward.

I don't want to see this. I don't want to see Lilah any other way but alive and smiling and teasing me about my stupid plans like she always does.

I don't want to see her dead.

But I need to.

I need to see her like that to convince myself this isn't just some horrible nightmare. Because my mind keeps telling me this is all too crazy to be real, and I'm struggling to keep hold of the truth anymore.

Is this only a nightmare? Am I still in a coma, twisting the words of the people talking in my room into vivid hallucinations?

I would take that nightmare over this one in a heartbeat.

I can just barely see over the casket's edge from my wheelchair when we near it. She's really in there, covered in makeup she would have never worn and looking more like a discarded mannequin than my best friend.

It's her. It's really, really her. But she's not the Lilah I remember.

This has to be a nightmare.

I snap my eyes closed, straining to hear the voices,

to hear Mom and Lilah telling me to wake up and that everything will be okay.

But no voices come. Not theirs, anyway. Just the murmur of people behind me, whispering about the girl who survived looking at the one who didn't.

An urgency in me takes over. I open my eyes and reach over the side of the casket, wanting to grab her hand. The tips of my fingers brush across her cold skin.

No mannequin. No hope for a nightmare I can wake from.

I lose it, wrenching my hand back and clutching it to my chest. Hysterical sobs consume me.

This is real.

Lilah is dead. My best friend is dead.

I don't understand why I'm not.

Dylan doesn't try to talk on the ride home from the cemetery. She finds my address in the folder Dr. Forsyth gave her and types it into the GPS, not bothering me for anything. I don't know that I'd be able to remember my address right now, anyway. I'm too numb to do more than breathe, and I feel guilty even doing that.

She parks in front of the house, not immediately

getting out. "There's a lot we need to talk about, but I'd like to get you in and settled for the night and worry about all that tomorrow, if that sounds good to you?"

Part of me wants to study her. To ask a million questions and learn everything I can about the aunt I was told I'd never want to know. But I'm too exhausted in every way to care about anything right now. Not even long lost family members that Mom will hate being in her home.

"Okay."

Dylan brings the wheelchair around and I struggle to push myself from the car to get into it. She's patient, but helps me.

She grabs the bag with my belongings and pulls out the keys to the house. "Which one, kiddo?" Dylan holds out the keyring and I point to the right one. She opens the door and pushes me inside.

Dylan moves around to stand in front of me. "I know you don't know me, and things are gonna be awkward for a bit. But, there's time for that later. I'm a nurse. Retired, but nurse all the same. I can tell you haven't had more than a sponge taken to you since you went into that hospital. I think a shower would do you good, if you're up for it?"

We have the same nose. She's my father's sister and

Mom hates her because of that. I know nothing else about her. But I'm drained in every way, and a shower sounds good.

I nod, modesty lost for the night.

"Now, you wait here just a sec. I'm gonna run out and grab your shower seat real quick. We'll worry about the rest later." She runs out the door and returns a few moments later with a plastic seat clearly made for showering. "Where's your bathroom?"

I point to the first door down the right side of the hall. Dylan takes the seat in and comes back for me shortly after.

"Hopefully, we won't be using this doo-dat long," Dylan gestures to the shower seat. "But it'll be helpful till your PT does its job."

I undress and she helps me onto the seat. She turns the water on, waiting until the temperature is right to pull the shower knob.

The water hits me and the feeling is immediate, the warm stream clearing my mind as it clears the grime from my body. I close my eyes and bring my hands up, feeling the water flow over my fingers and down my palms. I think I'm crying, but it doesn't matter. Everything washes away from me; the funeral, the hospital, the pain, the guilt, the bleak reality. It all washes away. I lose myself in that steady warmth and everything is alright for just a moment.

If only just that moment.

Dylan helps me finish my shower and get a quick dinner I can hardly eat before taking me to my bed. "I'll be bunking on the couch tonight, but you've got that button there that'll yell at me if you need anything, okay?" She points to a white remote with a single button on my nightstand. "I'm also a light sleeper, so I'll probably hear you before you even get it buzzing." She pauses before turning to leave. "I know this is weird for you, Ellessy. Hell, it's weird for me, too. But I'm here for the ride for as long as you need me and then some, kiddo. We'll get you through this."

She shuts off the light and closes the door halfway, leaving me to my thoughts. Lilah dances through them with Mom not far behind. The ache in my chest takes over, and I cry until I fall asleep.

Four

It's Monday. We spent the weekend going over Dylan's responsibilities and getting everything related to my recovery figured out.

As much as I hate to admit it, I like Dylan. She's older than Mom, somewhere in her sixties. She's built kinda big, which is nothing like how Mom described my father. Between her greyish brown hair and her sense of humor, she reminds me more of Mom than any of the few things I've heard about him. I guess that's a good thing.

Dylan is blunt charm with a touch of not-quite-southern sass. And we get along well. Just another reason to feel guilty when I have to tell Mom about this whole situation.

We haven't really discussed the whole "hey, we're

related" thing. I haven't brought it up yet and she, thankfully, hasn't pushed it. I've thought of so many questions I want to ask her, so many things I could never ask Mom, but I don't even know where to start. And, honestly, I'm not ready to find out she might really be as bad as her brother, anyway. I don't know her past. I don't know what she may have done.

Maybe... maybe I don't want to know?

She told me to tell her when I'm ready to talk about it, and, until then, to treat it however is comfortable. "Baby steps are still good steps," she said. So, baby steps it is.

That doesn't seem so bad to me.

"Are you ready?" I ask, watching Dylan throw my dirty laundry into a basket. I have my first physical therapy appointment today, and I'm anxious to get there. Number one on my plans to get better, and one step closer to being able to take care of myself before Mom wakes up.

Dylan chuckles. "Shouldn't I be asking you that?"

She digs through my dresser and tosses a tanktop and a sports bra at me. "Here, let's get you changed into these. You wanna wear something comfy and easy to move around in. Your leggings are fine, but you're gonna get hot in that t-shirt."

Dylan finds some socks and helps me where I need

it with getting changed. It's strange that I even need help with something so simple, but it took so much effort putting these leggings on by myself this morning that I don't even fight it.

She helps me into my wheelchair and we head to the kitchen where Dylan makes a quick breakfast. "Eat up, kiddo. Need food in that tummy before you can take your meds." She pushes a plate of waffles closer to me. "You want milk or juice?"

"Water," I say, quick to take another bite. Waffles have never tasted this good before. "What did you put in these?"

She hands me a glass of water. "Nothing. Pulled 'em out of a box."

"Well they're good. We need to buy more."

Dylan chuckles and preps my morning meds while I finish eating. "Bottoms up," she says, handing me a small handful of pills. I swallow them with the last of my water.

I hate having to take them at all. I've never been the type of person to bother with medicine if I can help it. I get it from Mom, who probably got it from seeing my father lose himself to drugs.

If I didn't absolutely need them to function right now, I wouldn't even bother.

"Alrighty, let's scoot. I want to get you there a little

early on day one." Dylan says, clearing the table. "I'll worry about these dishes later." She grabs my purse, tucking the paperwork I need for physical therapy inside, and hands it to me. "Now let's get you where you need to be."

Butterflies dance in my stomach as we pull up to the large, brick building. I have zero reference for basically anything physical. I didn't do sports in high school and I barely passed gym class. My determination doesn't hide the fact that I'm unprepared for this.

But I need it to work, and it needs to happen fast.

Dylan pushes me up to the front desk and tells the receptionist we're here for my appointment. The woman flashes us a bright smile and says, "Great! Louis is actually ready for you now, if you want to come on back." She stands and gestures for us to follow as she continues, "Right this way."

We head back to a room that reminds me of a gym, but much less intimidating. There are three doors along the back wall and we stop at the farthest one. The woman knocks twice and opens it.

It's a small office with a table in the middle rather than a desk. There's a younger guy sitting on the other side, and he stands when we come in, leaning forward with his arm outstretched to shake our hands. "You must be Ellessy." His voice matches the charming smile he gives with it.

"That, she is." Dylan says, squeezing my shoulder.

The woman who led us here leaves, closing the door behind her as she goes.

"Well, I'm excited to help you start your journey today. I'm Louis. And you must be?"

"Dylan. Just Dylan." She takes his hand, giving it a firm shake.

"Just Dylan, okay then." He smiles and sits back down, not asking any further questions about who she is to me. Instead, he pulls an open file on the table closer and says, "We're going to do a few exercises today, but we'll mostly be learning where you're at and what we need to work on, okay?"

The butterflies in my stomach start another lap. "Okay."

"Good." He looks at the file again. "Now, I see that you were recently in a car accident that left you partially paralyzed." Looking back up, he asks, "Is that right?"

I'm guessing the hospital sent him my records. I nod and mumble, "Yeah."

"And it's the left leg?" I nod again and he continues. "Alright, and I'm not seeing any other areas we need to focus on, correct? Just the one leg?"

"Thank God for that," Dylan says.

"My thoughts exactly."

Louis stands. He's got a body like a firefighter and his clothes aren't hiding it. One glance at Dylan tells me she notices, too. Or rather, that she catches *me* noticing. I can already tell this is going to be a long day.

Louis continues. "Well, we're mostly going to be doing some stretch exercises today. I want to see where we're at without giving your body more stress than necessary. Sound good?" He claps his hands together.

"Okay," I say. I look up at Dylan as Louis moves to the door. She gives me a nudge of encouragement, but the butterflies are still there.

We go to the far end of the bigger room, next to two parallel handrails and a stool. Louis helps me onto the stool and kneels down in front of me. "We're going to pop these off and take a look at what we're working with, okay?" He gestures to my shoes and I awkwardly shrug as he pulls them and my socks off and sets them to the side. "Alright, let's start easy. Wiggle your toes on both feet for me."

I focus. My brain sends the same command to both feet, but only my right toes wiggle. "Come on," I say, clearly frustrated. I try again, begging for even a flutter of movement. "They still won't do it."

"No worries, I'm just looking at what we're

working with for now. We'll focus on getting those toes going again once I've got an idea on where we need to start."

Louis lifts each of my legs and has me try to move my foot back and forth. Dylan swears she sees movement in my left foot, but I don't catch it.

We do the same thing with my knees. The left one bends, but it feels like there's an invisible pressure pushing against it.

"Okay, now lift your right leg and hold it up as long as you can. Leave this part limp." He taps the bottom of my leg. I lift my right leg with no issues. After about ten seconds, he taps my knee and says, "Good, now the other one."

I lift my left leg, feeling the weight of my paralysis fighting against me. I furrow my brows, chewing on my cheek and gripping the edge of the seat.

My leg drops before five seconds are up.

"Good! That's awesome, Ellessy. You're doing great." Louis claps his hands together as if I've just accomplished something big. I don't really feel like I've done anything with celebrating.

"I couldn't hold it up."

"I just watched you hold it up." He smiles and turns to Dylan. "Did you see her hold up that leg?"

"I sure did."

"See? That's two witnesses. I'd say you did it."

I fight the grin pulling at one corner of my mouth. "I didn't do it very long, though..."

"I said to hold it as long as you could, and you did that. We celebrate all the wins here, Ellessy." He holds up his hand, waiting for me to high-five him.

I give in.

"Let me get one of those, too," Dylan says, holding her own hand up in front of me.

Louis swoops in and smacks it before I can, a cheeky smile following after. Dylan wiggles her hand, not taking it back until I give her a high-five, too.

We spend the rest of the appointment working with colored resistance bands, Louis holding one side while I pull my leg against it.

It feels like I'm hardly doing anything, but I still leave the appointment exhausted. Louis says it's all to be expected, but that doesn't keep me from feeling discouraged.

I need to get better faster than this.

"We need to get some groceries on the way home, if that's okay?" Dylan asks as she pulls away from the building.

"That's fine."

"Can't go having you run out of your waffles, can we?"

I turn away from the window and give her a weak smile. I know she can tell I'm in my thoughts, and I'm thankful she doesn't push.

There's a grocery store close to home. It's not a huge place, but it has all the necessities for a decent price. Considering I'm paying for everything with my college savings right now, good prices are pretty important.

Dylan talked to me about temporary disability over the weekend, but I don't want to apply. I don't think I need to. I'm determined to get back to normal as soon as possible. Besides, my job at the bookstore isn't hard, and I know it's waiting for me when I'm ready to come back. Dylan already called to make sure.

Until then, dipping into the college fund Mom and I have been adding to for the past ten years will have to do.

Dylan has also been helping out, of course. But I'm doing what I can to keep that help at a minimum. We haven't talked about her source of income, but I know she retired recently. I have no clue what kind of income that leaves her, but I don't intend to ask–or expect her to use it on me.

"Alright, kiddo. I've got toilet paper, dish soap, laundry detergent, your waffles, butter, bread, and syrup on my list. Figured we might as well knock it all out while we're here." Dylan looks over the notepad in her hand. "Anything else we need? You good on tampons and all that?"

I shake my head. "I'm good for now... But you're out of coffee, aren't you?"

Her eyes widen. "Well if you didn't just save the day." Dylan pulls a pen out of the pocket on her blue jean shirt and scribbles something on her list.

She pushes me over to a stack of baskets and holds one out to me. "Mind being the cart today?"

"I think I can manage that." I grin and take the basket to hold in my lap. It's kinda nice to feel useful for a change.

We head down the aisles at a quick pace. We don't need much and apparently neither of us like to spend more time than necessary shopping.

It only takes about ten minutes to grab everything, lucky to get here at a time when it isn't too busy. Dylan steers us into an empty checkout lane and unloads the basket.

"Did y'all find everything okay?" The cashier smiles extra big and does her best to avoid looking anywhere below my neck.

"We did, thank you." Dylan says.

"Good! Good, I'm glad to hear that." Her eyes flick to my wheelchair for just a moment before meeting mine. Her cheeks turn red and she tears her attention away, focusing on bagging our stuff.

My shoulders slump. I look around, catching other eyes from people hastily pretending they weren't staring, too.

Should I pretend I didn't notice?

She gives Dylan our total and cashes out the transaction. "Y'all have a *wonderful* night!" She emphasises the word more than necessary. Will the couple in line behind us be offered the same amount of wonderful as the girl in the wheelchair?

Dylan doesn't waste time getting me out of there.

We jump on my bed, giggling and reading our acceptance letters like a couple of kids rather than young women holding the keys to their future.

My left leg gives out, and I drop to the bed, but Lilah keeps reading her letter aloud. "Dear Ms. Lilah Day, we are pleased to inform you that we have accepted your admission to Oakvale University..." She doesn't seem to notice that I'm not jumping with her anymore.

"Something is wrong," I tell her, a weird pressure forming in my head.

Mom leans against the doorway. "You break that

bed, and you'll have to add buying a new one to your plans." Lilah keeps jumping.

The pressure grows, feeling more like a dark cold as it snakes its way through my body.

"Are you girls ready?" Mom asks. "I don't want to get to Goodwin's in the middle of their rush."

Dread consumes me. "I don't think we should go."

"We have to," Lilah says as she hops down from the bed.

"I think something bad is going to happen, Lilah." I glance at Mom, but she just smiles like everything is okay.

Lilah shrugs and grabs her purse, repeating herself, her smile still in place. "We have to."

My whole body trembles and tears spill over. "I don't think you'll make it if we go." The words come out like vomit, my stomach empty and throat aching as they spill from my mouth.

Lilah walks over to Mom and kisses her on the cheek. She pauses next to her, taking her hand and turning to look at me once more to say, "We have to." She turns without a sound and walks down the hallway, her fingertips leaving Mom's hand being the last I see of her.

"Are you ready, Little Elle?" Mom asks, holding that same hand out to me.

"You don't understand, Mom, you have to go get

her! We have to stay here! I promise you, something bad is going to happen if we go!" My panicked shouts don't do a thing to budge the smile on Mom's face.

I try to get up so I can run after Lilah, but my leg won't work and I tumble off the bed, jerking my body back to the waking world.

Panting, heart pounding, I glance around the room, looking for anything to tell me it wasn't a dream and I can go chasing after them.

My wheelchair is all I need to see to shatter the irrational hope I was clinging to.

I slowly lie back down, feeling the sweat on my neck and scalp as my pillow pushes my hair against them.

I don't yell for Dylan right away. I can hear her banging around in the kitchen, singing to herself as she works. She sounds so happy and full of life, even being away from her home, caring for the niece she barely knows, knowing she'll be kicked out when Mom wakes up. She lets everything run off her shoulders.

She's really given this place some warmth during... all this.

Yet, even with her just down the hall, I feel incredibly alone.

The corners of my mouth tug down and I can't fight the tears. The dark feeling from my dream slithers over me like a heavy blanket that I'm too weak to push off. All motivation is gone.

I stare at the ceiling as the tears stream down the sides of my face, sliding across my cheeks and into my ears. It's uncomfortable, but I can't bring myself to wipe them away, either because I don't care or because I don't have the strength to do anything other than wallow.

Footsteps and humming draw closer to my room. Dylan pokes her head inside.

"Oh, kiddo..." She frowns and moves over to my bed, grabbing the tissues off my nightstand as she sits next to me. She wipes the tears away, continuing to hum quietly as she does.

I close my eyes and listen to her melody until the tears stop coming.

Dylan moves a piece of hair that's stuck to my cheek aside, her voice soft as she says, "You wanna go see your mom?"

I nod, squeezing my eyes closed tighter to keep the tears from starting again.

Dylan gives me a moment to collect myself as she stands and pulls my wheelchair over. Then she helps me into it and hands me a pair of house slippers. Winking, she says, "Might as well go comfy. Who's gonna say anything, right?"

I want to smile, but my mouth barely gives in. Still, I'm thankful for these moments with her, where she treats me like a human who needs some humor and not a girl who's lost nearly everything.

Dylan sings to the radio on the way. Old rock, like usual. The same music Mom listens to. Another thing they have in common.

Déjà vu hits me at that thought, and I feel uncomfortable for some reason. I frown, doing my best to keep my thoughts quiet for the rest of the ride.

I let Dylan do the talking all the way up to Mom's room. Nurses that remember me try to ask how I'm doing, but she pushes me along without stopping, telling them we're "crunching time". It's nice that they care, but visiting hours only last so long.

Dylan pushes me over to the bed and steps back, her voice quiet as she says, "I'll be in the hallway, kiddo."

I listen for her footsteps to stop outside the door before I do anything. If Mom knew they had been in the same room together, she'd be livid.

Maybe I should ask Dylan to come back? Maybe it would wake Mom up?

My shoulders slump a little. I can't wait for Mom to wake up, but even if I get better and send Dylan away before she does, I'll still have to tell her she was here.

I roll a little closer to the bed, doing my best to leave the guilt behind me for the moment.

Mom doesn't look much different than last time. The swelling has gone down and the bruising is a different color, but she's still got a breathing tube and that central line thing. It's so hard seeing her like this.

My voice cracks as I try to speak to her. I clear my throat and try again. "Mom, it's me, Little Elle." I slide my hand into hers and squeeze. My lower lip starts to tremble and I chew on my cheek to stop it.

None of that right now. Not here.

I clear my throat again, determined to do this right. If she might really be able to hear me, I want her to hear me how she remembers.

"I went to my first physical therapy appointment. My, uh... my physical therapist looks like a firefighter." I wait for her to crack a smile, to make a joke about Lilah corrupting me for sure, but her lips don't move.

I trace my fingers along hers as I tell her about physical therapy and my weird cravings and how ready I am to get back to work, the awkwardness of the situation seeming to fade from my voice as I keep talking. Nothing feels right about this, of course, but I find it easier to speak into the silence of Mom's hospital room. Which isn't really silent, anyway, with all the machines keeping her alive.

The thought stumbles from my mind and I slap my hand to my mouth, even though I never spoke the words.

Keeping her alive.

That's not what's happening here.

I jerk as a hand touches my shoulder. "It's just me, Elle," Dylan says. "The nurses need your mom's attention for a bit. What say we grab some food, huh?"

There's a nurse waiting in the doorway. She waves and I give her a weak smile before turning back to Mom. I lean in and pull her hand to my face, pressing my cheek into her soft skin before kissing it. "I love you, Mom. I love you so much." One more kiss to her palm and then we leave.

Keeping her alive.

The intrusive thought worms its way back into the center of my mind.

The room suddenly feels so small. Or maybe the walls are bigger than they're supposed to be. "Dylan..." I try to move myself backward, but my hands fumble with the wheels.

Her footsteps sound like cannons firing. I close my eyes and cover my ears. Dylan is saying something, but

I can't focus on the words. There's a weird pressure in my head, like there's too much happening in it with no room.

"Dylan, something's wrong." Nothing feels real right now. I can't breathe. I can't remember how.

"Ellessy." Her words are muffled or maybe my heart is beating too loud? "I need you to listen to my voice. Can you hear me?"

The pressure in my head is so loud. "Dylan?"

"Yes, Elle, I'm here. Can you look at me?" I open my eyes. Dylan is kneeling in front of me. She takes my hand and puts her fingers to my wrist. "Good. Okay, now I want you to tell me what you see around the room that's blue. Can you do that?"

I don't understand but I cling to her words, looking around for anything blue, trusting she knows how to pull me back from whatever this is. "Curtain... blanket... ink pen." My breathing starts to calm. The pressure starts to fade. "The lamp. The border on the wall." My heart slowly stops trying to escape my chest.

"Okay, Elle, that's good." Dylan lets go of my wrist.

Exhaustion hits me as fast as this all came on. "I think I'm ready for bed now."

"I'd say so. You just had a panic attack." Dyan

gently pats my knee and stands. "Let's get you home, kiddo."

Panic attacks. One more thing added to the list.

Five

We're on day four of waffles for breakfast, and Dylan is finding it hilarious.

I've had intense cravings for those and onion rings since coming home. And I mean intense. They're basically all I want to eat. Dylan suggested it could be a side-effect of my brain injury. All I know is that nothing sounds or tastes as good as they do right now.

Dylan chuckles over her coffee as I finish the last few bites on my plate.

"Do you have anything planned for us today?" I ask.

"Whatever you're itching for." She turns a page in her newspaper. "Is there something you were wantin' to do?"

I lean back, wiping some dripped syrup from my mouth.

I had physical therapy yesterday and I'm still feeling it. Louis had me work with the exercise bands again, which I don't feel like I'm making nearly enough progress with. He also reminded me to practice wiggling my toes at home. So far, they won't budge. But at least I'm slowly getting closer to not using the wheelchair anymore.

I glance at the wheelchair next to me as I push my empty plate to the side. I've been moving myself from my chair into seats regularly, but standing isn't an option yet.

I'll get there. I have to. That's number one on my plans, now: get out of this wheelchair.

"Did you still want to stop by the bookstore?" Dylan asks. She turns another page in her paper, not seeming to notice how lost I'd been in my thoughts.

I sigh.

I haven't been reading much lately. My mind won't stay focused long enough to take in the words, and my memory is still so rough that I can't keep track of what I've already covered. The only thing that I've been able to enjoy is poetry–giving me an escape without asking too much of my rattled brain.

Unfortunately, I've gone through all of the poetry books I have.

"Yeah, if we can," I say.

"It's whatever you want, kiddo."

It's hard for me to admit it, but I'm really thankful to have Dylan here. Even when I'm feeling like I have been lately, she still manages to offer a little light in the darkness.

Which makes me sad, too. Mom hates Dylan so much that she kept me from knowing her all these years, didn't even want a mention of her.

What's going to happen when Mom wakes up?

I haven't been to the bookshop since before my accident. I love my job. I've always been a book lover and I was ecstatic when Rob and Martha hired me on. It's not a big store by any means, with only two employees outside of the owner, but it's pretty popular. Rob always says this place is "everybody's favorite book store". I don't think he's wrong. At least not locally.

I was working weekends during the school year, but since graduating, I've been working through the week, too. Rob and Martha even said they'd work around my college schedule, so the job has honestly been a dream come true.

I guess I should say it *was* a dream come true. College isn't much of a worry anymore.

I wave Dylan away as she tries to push my wheelchair up to the bookshop. I can't expect to get better any faster if I'm not putting in the effort on my own.

A little girl points at me. "Mommy, why does that girl have a thing like grandma?"

"Shh, I don't know, sweetie," her mom whispers, pushing her hand down. They both stare.

I expect it from the kids. I'm learning to expect it from everyone. I know it looks weird seeing someone my age use a wheelchair, but shouldn't the adults know how much it hurts when they stare? Take your glimpse and move on.

Dylan holds the door to the book shop open for me and I do my best to hurry inside.

"Ellessy!" A booming voice comes from the back of the store. Rob walks toward me with his arms ready to throw one of his bear hugs my way. "Boy, am I glad to see you doing so well. The news didn't paint a pleasant picture and when Ms. Dylan called us about your job, well..." his voice trails off. "We're just glad to see you're keeping on." He smiles and shoves his hands in his pockets, giving up on the hug.

"Thank you, Rob." It comes out as a mumble, though I really do mean it.

"Hey, uh, don't you worry about your job, either. Abbie picked up the extra hours when Martha and I couldn't, and the new hire has caught on quick. Your job will be here whenever you're ready to come back. No rush. Just let us know and we'll work with you, no problem."

"See that, kiddo? No worries here. Plenty of time to rest and get that leg back into gear." Dylan squeezes my shoulder. If only time wasn't an issue.

"Is that who I think it is?" Martha appears from the back of the store. "I thought I heard Rob getting excited over something, and now I see why." She comes over and leans into him. "It's good to see you, Elle. Rob and I were just talking about you, actually." She smiles in that way that people do when they know you've been through a lot.

"Oh, I'm glad you said something," Rob says. "Elle, we want to put together an auction for you and your mom. To help with things, you know?"

An auction?

"You won't have to fiddle with any of the details," Martha says. "We'll handle everything that goes into it. We just wanted to make sure you're okay with it." She brings her hands together against her chest, a warm smile waiting patiently on her face for my answer.

I look up at Dylan. "That's up to you, kiddo." She

shrugs but adds, "But I've always said that there's nothin' wrong with letting people help every now and then."

Part of me wants to tell them "no," to say that they didn't need to do something so big. But I don't know how long I can keep pulling from my college savings, and I don't want Dylan doing any more than she already is. So, maybe she's right?

And I can also see this is something they really want to do. "Yeah, okay."

"Wonderful!" Rob pulls away from Martha. "Honey, would you want to go back and start making calls?"

"Absolutely." Martha winks at me and heads to the back room.

"I'll let you know all the details when we've got them all tacked down," Rob says.

"Sounds good," Dylan tells him. She turns to me and asks, "You ready to go look at books, kiddo?"

I nod and Rob leaves us to it.

We reach the poetry section and I start pulling books from the shelf. The covers are pretty and they aren't ones I've read, so I hand them to Dylan to carry for me. "Guess *I'm* the basket this time around." She chuckles. I can't help but grin.

I plan to read through these pretty fast, so I keep looking, pulling anything that catches my eye.

"Finding everything alright?" I look up. A guy around my age is standing in front of me. He picks a book from the shelf I'd been looking at and holds it out. "Have you read this one? It's one of my favorites." He smiles at me.

"I haven't." I take the book, eyeing him carefully as I do. He's not staring at my wheelchair. He's not really staring at me, either, just looking at me like I'm any other customer rather than a teenage girl who can't walk.

"I think I've read it a few times, actually. It's the book that got me into poetry." He scratches at the back of his neck, his smile seeming suddenly shy.

Dylan clears her throat. I glance at her, ignoring the look she gives me, and turn my eyes back to the book in my hand. It's a collection of winning poems sent in for a contest. They make a new one every year. I actually have a few of the older ones at home. "I'll give it a shot." I hand the book to Dylan.

His eyes seem to twinkle. "Awesome! I know you'll like it. I mean, I can't imagine anyone who wouldn't..." His voice trails off as Rob comes up behind him and gives his back a friendly smack, causing him to stumble a step forward.

"I see you've met Ellessy." Rob's voice booms across the store, as always.

The guy standing in front of me has an obvious moment of realization. "Oh! I've heard so much about you." He holds his hand out. "I'm Milo."

"He's the new hire," Rob says.

He's the person filling in for me while I'm gone. Knowing Rob, he'll stay on long after I come back. "Ellessy," I say, putting my hand in his. His handshake seems to match his personality.

"You probably know this store front to back, and here I am trying to help you pick out books." He gives an awkward laugh, red tinting his cheeks.

"I think Milo is gonna be part of the 'Rob and Martha's' family for good," Rob pats Milo's shoulder again. "I'm sure you two will get on well when you're ready to come back." He flashes a toothy smile and adds, "No rush, though. We're ready for you when you're ready for us." He turns his attention to Dylan and asks, "Could I steal you for a minute? I want to run a few things by you concerning the auction."

"Do you want me to ring you up?" Milo gestures to the stack of books Dylan is holding. "I can take those."

"I think we've probably got enough here, kiddo.

We throw any more on this stack and we're gonna end up looking lopsided on the drive home."

"Yeah, I think we're ready."

"I'm gonna hand these off to you, then," Dylan says, handing the stack to Milo.

"We'll only be a few," Rob says. "Will you be okay without us?"

"She can holler if she needs me," Dylan says, giving me a wink that really isn't subtle at all.

I follow Milo to the register as Dylan disappears into the back with Rob.

"Which one are you going to read first?" Milo begins ringing up the books.

"Huh? Oh. I don't know." I watch him carefully, waiting for his eyes to flick to my chair as he scans. Just like the woman and her kid in the parking lot. Just like the cashier at the grocery store.

"I'm super biased, but I recommend this one." He wiggles the book he picked out earlier.

"I'll keep that in mind."

He grins and places it in the bag. "Nothing wrong with reading one of the other ones first, though. Books are books and reading is reading, right? Well..." He frowns, looking off to the side. "Unless it's a problematic book. Or a problematic author."

"I tend to avoid those if I can help it."

He looks at me, his smile back in place. "Same."

"Get everything good and sorted?" Dylan asks, startling us both as she returns. "Whoops, didn't mean to scare y'uns."

"No problem," Milo says, blushing again. "I scare really easy." He scans the last book and makes sure to put my employee discount on before giving us the total. Dylan hands him some money, waving away my attempts to pay.

"I'm glad I finally got to meet you." His eyes meet mine again, not a single glance toward the wheelchair.

"Thanks," I mumble. Does he really not notice it? Does he really not care?

"Alright, kiddo, let's get you home." Dylan grabs the bag of books and helps me out of the store. I'm not even buckled in before she asks, "That Milo was a cutie, right?"

I look out the window, hiding the blush I know is on my own face this time.

She's not wrong. But I feel like I shouldn't be thinking about it. Not when every other part of my life is upside down right now.

It's not in the plans.

"I think I need a nap," I say, hoping she'll drop the subject.

Dylan chuckles. "Uh-huh."

Six

"Who is he, Ellessy?" Lilah points at the guy across the room from us. "Is he worth it?"

"Is he worth it? What are you talking about, Lilah?"

"Your heart. Is he worth your heart?" She gives me that look she always gives when I ask questions she deems *"too stupid for a smart girl like me."*

I look over at him again, knitting my brows together. "I have no clue what you're talking about. I don't even know that guy."

She turns my face back to look at her, holding my chin in place. "Elle. You gotta find something that's worth it. Your heart isn't going to stay together, sis. You better make sure you've got something worth it when the *damn thing falls apart."* She lightly taps her knuckles under my chin before pulling her hand back.

"What is wrong with you, Lilah? I don't know what has you talking like this or who that guy is." I gesture to him, but he's gone. I look back at Lilah, and she's gone, too.

Something dark starts building in my chest. I stumble backward. Something isn't right. Those words feel like déjà vu in my head.

Something isn't right.

Everything starts spinning. I clutch my head with both hands, as if holding onto myself will keep me from falling away.

"What's happening?"

I open my mouth to scream and the sound that comes out of me sends chills down my own spine, echoing around me.

How did I get here? Where is Lilah? What on Earth is going on?

I close my eyes and listen to the pounding of my heart growing louder and louder, becoming the only sound I can hear.

BOOM. BOOM. BOOM. BOOM.

"Did you fall asleep reading, Elle?" I jerk awake at the sound of Dylan's voice, sucking in a breath on a violent motion that makes her jump, too.

I try to suck in another breath, but I feel like I can't breathe. I keep trying, the room spinning with every gasp.

Dylan grabs my shoulders. "Breathe, Elle. You gotta look at me and breathe." She leans in so that I'm forced to look at her. "Breathe with me."

She takes a slow breath in, moving her hands up as her chest rises and down as she slowly releases the breath.

"I can't." I continue to gasp for air, but it feels like nothing is making its way to my lungs.

"Yes, you can. Count with me," Dylan says, grabbing my hand and placing it on her chest as she breathes in, slowly counting to five. "Good, now breathe out." She counts to five again as she exhales. We do it over and over until the room stands still again. And then we sit there in silence, still breathing to the count of five, but no words passing between us.

"Water," I finally say, sitting up.

Dylan runs to the kitchen, the fastest I think I've ever seen her move, and returns with a glass of water. "Still having nightmares?"

I close my eyes and nod, drinking almost the entire glass-full.

"I'm sorry, kiddo," Dylan pats my knee. "I'm prayin' they won't last for you."

So am I.

She stands again, grabbing the books I'd fallen asleep with. "Did he have good taste?"

"Huh?"

She wiggles one of the books. "Isn't this the one ol' Milo picked out for you?"

I roll my eyes, leaning over to snatch the books away from her. "Yes, but I haven't read it yet."

She smiles. "Uh-huh." I turn and set the books back in the bag with the others, feeling a warmth in my cheeks that I don't care to show. "Your meds are on the table, extra pain pills optional. You can always take it later if you need it."

I'm not sure what my tolerance is like with addictive pain medications, and I'm not looking to test the limits. "I think I'll pass on it for now." Or forever, if I can help it.

Dylan stares at me like she knows where my thoughts are going. "You aren't your father, Elle. It's okay to take care of yourself." I start to say something and she stops me, continuing, "I'm not gonna push you to take pain meds just 'cause you're in pain or anything. But I don't want you being in pain just because you're afraid of being him, okay?"

I let her words sink in, slowly nodding. I reach over

and grab just my regular meds from the table. "Thank you."

She scoops up the remaining pill. "We've got physical therapy today, so I'll bring it with us and you can let me know how you're feeling after. Sound good?"

"Sounds good." Half my mouth turns up in a grin and I ask, "Waffles first?"

Dylan smiles. "Waffles first, kiddo."

We're working on the parallel handrails again today. Louis says that if things go like he expects, I'll be leaving my appointment with a walker instead of a wheelchair.

Part of me is excited and proud that I've gotten this far in only a few weeks, but the reality of using a walker at eighteen is still a hard one to adjust to.

"Just a few more steps, you've got this," Louis says, gesturing for me to keep moving forward. I make it to the end of the handrails and he cheers with more enthusiasm than necessary. "How did it feel? Do you think we can do one more?"

I nod, not waiting for him to help me turn around, gritting my teeth through the ache and doing it myself instead.

The second walk along the handrails is hard, but my adrenaline pushes me faster than before.

Breathless, I finally match Louis' enthusiasm. "I did it!" I lift one arm up for the high five I know is coming.

Louis wastes no time smacking his hand to mine. "I think it might be time to retire that wheelchair. What do you say?"

My jaw drops. "Really?" Please tell me it's really happening.

All that time at home, staring at my foot, trying so hard to make it move or get my toes to wiggle with only the tiniest results, the times we worked on the handrails and I could barely make it halfway without needing a break, every little bit of work we've put in, and it feels like it's all finally paying off.

Louis looks over to Dylan. "I think we're ready for it."

She tosses her magazine to the side and stands. "I'll be right back." She runs toward the lobby and disappears.

I grip the handrails a little tighter, so ready for this. *No more wheelchair.* After only a few weeks of physical therapy, I'm walking again.

Not without help, but still. We celebrate all the wins here, right?

I can't wait to tell Mom.

Dylan returns and sets a walker down in front of me. Louis holds out his hand and helps me over to it. "Do you think you've got the energy to make it to the lobby?" he asks.

"Only one way to find out," Dylan says.

The steps are awkward, but I make it, Dylan and Louis following and cheering behind me. Any other day, I'd be embarrassed.

Not today. This is a huge thing marked off the list and a big step closer to–

I let the thought falter, not wanting to spoil the moment.

"One more high five and I think we can call it a day," Louis says. I turn and give him one, seeing that Dylan has my wheelchair as I do. Louis points at it. "I want you to keep that just in case. I know you're a rockstar who probably won't need it, but we want to be smart about this, right?"

"Smart like a stubborn crawfish." Dylan grins and I can't help but grin with her at the phrase.

"We'll see you next week, Ellessy." Louis gets another high five from Dylan before walking back to his office.

We head out to the SUV, excitement pushing every step. Dylan helps me into the passenger seat and stows my wheelchair and walker in the back. "You up for some food?"

"Yeah, I could go for some onion rings." My new food obsession.

"How did I know you were gonna say that?" She chuckles and starts the SUV. "We'll go in and eat since we've got somethin' to celebrate. Sound good?"

Lilah's words hit my mind on a shiver and I suck in a breath.

I thought we were celebrating?

"You okay, kiddo?" Dylan asks, the grin fading from her face.

I shake my head. "Yeah… uh, cold chill."

She hesitates, seeming to pick up on the shift in mood, but only for a moment.

We get to the fast food place and I sit while Dylan gets our food.

I try not to think about the guilt washing over me. It hasn't even been a month since Lilah di–since the accident, and I'm out celebrating something. With someone that Mom hates.

Maybe it's time to have that conversation?

Dylan sets the tray on our table and sits across from me. I wait until everything is separated, then ask, "Why does Mom hate you?" It feels like a dumb question, but I don't know how else to start.

Dylan sets her burger down. "How much do you know about your dad?"

"Not much. I know he overdosed." Talking about him leaves a bad taste in my mouth.

"Nothing before that?" she asks. I shake my head and she continues. "Well, I was nineteen and out of the house when he was born."

"Wow." It's clear Dylan is older than Mom, but the age difference never really registered with me like this.

"Yeah, I don't think the parents planned on him makin' an appearance." She chuckles and takes a drink of her soda. "I don't know what made him get started with drugs, but he was younger than you are now."

"Wait, he was on drugs when he met my mom?" And she still gave him the time of day?

"I don't think she knew, Elle. They weren't together very long and he died right after she told him she was pregnant."

No wonder Mom won't talk about him. She didn't even know it was all a lie until it was too late.

I pick at my food. "Why didn't you tell her? That he was on drugs."

"I didn't meet your mom till the cops were calling. Didn't even know they'd been a thing."

I stiffen on a chill. "What do you mean?" Was Mom there when he died? As far as I knew, she caught him doing drugs and that was it—she left and never looked back.

Dylan eyes me for a moment, as if she's hesitant to continue. "Your mama really didn't tell you what happened?"

"No." And I'm not sure how I feel about it.

"I don't know if it's my place to tell you stuff, Elle."

"Please. I want to know." What didn't Mom tell me?

Dylan sighs and takes a long drink before she says, "The morning after your mom told him she was pregnant, she woke up and found him dead."

Everything stands still.

"Mom found him?"

"She did."

She didn't even have a chance to leave him. He was gone before she even knew.

Everything I thought I knew about that moment is wrong. "What happened?"

"She called the cops and they called me when they couldn't get through to our parents." There's a bitterness in her voice when she mentions them. "I left work and drove over and your mom... oh, she was hysterical."

I want so much to reach into her memories and see it myself.

Dylan pauses a moment before pressing on. "She

asked if I knew and why I didn't help him get clean. But you can't help someone who doesn't want help, and I told her that. So she told me to stay out of your lives."

"She told you she was pregnant?" Dylan knew about me. Another thing I'm not sure how to feel about.

"She said 'stay away from *us*' and I connected the dots."

My voice is quiet. "Why didn't you try?"

"It's not that I didn't want to, kiddo. But I wasn't gonna disrespect her decision. Especially not after what she went through."

"She thought you'd be like him, too." I know my mom well enough to make the guess.

"Something 'bout an apple and a tree, right?" Dylan chuckles. "She wasn't wrong, really. Our parents weren't much to sing praises about, either. Hell, call me the black sheep if you want."

My eyes widen when she mentions their parents. I hadn't even thought about having grandparents out there. "What about them? Your parents, I mean. Are they?"

"Alive?" She shakes her head. "No. They were getting old when they had your dad. Died old, too. Just a few years ago."

"So there's no one else?" No one else Mom might have been wrong about?

"No one worth it, kiddo." Dylan reaches forward and squeezes my hand. "I'm afraid I'm all the lost family you're gonna get." She winks and gets up to throw away our trash.

I lean back in my chair. I've never really been that curious about my father or his family before. It's always just been me and Mom and Lilah and I've never felt like I needed anything more. Mom talks like his side of the family is all bad, so why would I be curious?

But she's wrong. Dylan isn't like the rest of them. I really think she isn't bad at all.

If Mom had only given her a chance, things could have been so different.

Mark off "get out of the wheelchair" and add "help Mom see who Dylan really is" to my plans, I guess.

Dylan returns, sitting across from me again. "You have any other questions, kiddo?"

I think about it for only a second, the other big thing that's been nagging at me tumbling out before I can stop it. "Why did you agree to come help me?"

She smiles like the answer should be obvious. "You're family." She leans forward and adds, "And you're also your mother's daughter."

I tilt my head, scrunching my brows together.

"What do you mean?" Wouldn't that be something that should turn her away?

She shrugs like she doesn't know how else to say what she means. "She told me to stay out of your life because she thought there was a chance I might be anything like your dad. Now that tells me that she's a good woman and a better mother." Dylan smiles. "Besides, I've been bored as hell since retiring. Nothin' like a bit of long, lost family to get the wheels turning again."

I bite the slow grin that forms.

My heart aches a little that I never got to know her as the aunt she is, that Mom never let me.

Mom.

Worry replaces that ache. She is so strong willed and holds fast to her grudges, especially this one.

"Mom isn't going to be happy when she wakes up," I say. I have no doubt she'll be simultaneously thankful that someone was there for me and angry that the someone was Dylan. And angrier still that *I'm* the one who asked her to come. Or maybe disappointed. Or probably both.

Dylan waves it away. "Oh, she'll be angry with me at some point, sure. But not at first. She's just going to be happy as hell that you're alright. I bet the devil himself could have come up and taken care of you and her first thought would still be how thankful she is that you're doin' alright and there was someone here who made sure of it."

I frown, realization setting in. "I'll have to tell her about Lilah."

"And that's another reason why she's not gonna be too bothered by me to start." Dylan tucks some hair behind my ear. "You don't need to worry yourself over this, Elle. Everything is gonna work out fine. Your mama is gonna be so darn happy to see you standing there next to her, that's all that's gonna matter."

"Yeah, maybe..." I shake my head, trying to shake the worry away with it.

"Trust me, kiddo. I've maybe seen it a time or two or five." She stands and checks her watch. "Well, as much as I enjoy getting to know each other and all, I didn't bring your meds with me and it's about that time. You ready to go home?"

"Yeah," I say, pulling my walker close to me. "Let's go home."

Seven

Some days are harder than others and today is one of them.

We went to get my staples taken out this morning. The nurse told me it wouldn't hurt, but the skin had grown over some of them. It felt like what I imagined having staples pulled out of my head would feel like. And it wasn't good.

I don't want to get out of bed or take my pain meds, even though my head is pounding. I don't want to use any effort to do anything other than breathe, and even that feels like it's too much.

I want my mom. I want Lilah. I want my body back to normal and my life back the way it used to be.

I'm angry. And it floods my veins like liquid fire.

"Elle?" Dylan knocks softly on my bedroom door. "You need anything, kiddo?"

I stay quiet for a long time. What is there that could help me right now? "I don't know," I tell her.

Dylan leaves the room and returns a few moments later with a glass of water. She also sets a pill on the desk. "No shame if you need it. No pressure if you don't."

She doesn't wait for me to respond, closing the door to a crack as she leaves.

I sit up and grab the glass of water and take a long drink.

"Dylan?" I call, just loud enough for her to hear.

She's back in my doorway in seconds. "What do you need?"

I grab the pill and hold it up. "Do you think we could cut this in half or something? Isn't that a thing?"

"It sure is and we sure can." Dylan takes the pill from me and leaves the room, returning a moment later with it neatly cut in two. "Here you go, kiddo."

"Thank you."

"You need anything else?" she asks. I shake my head. She closes the door to a crack again, saying, "Just let me know."

I swallow the half she gave me and set the glass of water back on the desk when I'm done. Then I drop my head back into my pillow, feeling like a heaviness has dropped down with me.

It's not fair. None of this is. Lilah is–*was* a kid. Mom hasn't even lived half a lifetime yet, and she's missing the moments I need her most. And if she doesn't wake up... well, I can't even think about that. Because that can't happen. I cannot imagine a life without her, can't even fathom it. Especially not on top of everything else that has already happened.

I just don't understand why.

Why Lilah? Why Mom? Why not me? The same questions over and over.

I close my eyes and rub my temples, that pounding in my head not seeming to want to go away.

Today I get to be angry. I get to stay in bed and sleep and cry and ignore everything else.

I've been fighting so hard to get better, don't I deserve a day to wallow and be mad?

The anger in me flares up again.

Why is this real? Why is this my life right now? When am I going to wake up and find out that it was all a nightmare and everything is really okay?

I know the answers to these questions, but my mind keeps asking–keeps begging–for a different reply.

It isn't fair. Words you'd think were tattooed to the inside of my eyelids as much as they flash through my mind. But they're true. It isn't fair. None of this is and my mind can't wrap itself around any of it.

My phone vibrates on the desk. I accept the distraction and pick it up.

> Hey, this is Milo! Rob asked me to text you and remind you about the fundraiser for you and your mom. I hope you don't mind… he didn't want to call and said he doesn't do the text thing so he gave me your number.

I read through it again. I'm not at all surprised that Rob would ask someone else to text for him.

My mind is so jumbled, I'm not even sure what to say.

> The auction?

Milo's reply comes quick.

> Yeah! Rob and Martha have a bunch of overstock books in the back that they weren't sure what to do with. They thought those would be perfect for it. Plus they got a bunch of other people and businesses to donate too.

My heart swells a little. That couple has treated me like family since my first day working at their shop.

> I appreciate their kindness. Have they picked a date for it?

I feel thankful and awkward at the same time. It's weird being in a position where people want to help you, even if I'm thankful for the help.

> They've got it set up for this Saturday, but weren't sure if that would be too soon for you. They said to tell you it's okay if you can't make it.

I look at the calendar app on my phone. Saturday is only a few days away. Really short notice. But that's Ron and Martha for you. They get ahead of themselves and forget things like that sometimes.

> Saturday is good for me.

Another quick reply.

> Awesome! I'll see you Saturday then! :)

I set my phone down without responding. Today is not a day for smiley faces.

My phone vibrates again.

> Soo… how are you?

Milo's message sits patiently on the screen.

> I'm alive.

What else can I say without taking my anger out on him?

> Well that's a good thing lol

I can't even bring myself to smile.

> Right.

I set my phone down again, ready to ignore any more messages from the guy who didn't stare. One more comes through and curiosity nags me enough to read it.

> Well if you ever need to talk, I'm always here. I'll see you Saturday. Hope the rest of your day is awesome :)

It takes everything in me not to be angry at him as much as I am thankful for the kindness. My day isn't awesome and it won't be awesome. It's not his fault, I know, but my mind doesn't care right now.

I toss my phone to the floor. It's probably safer for everyone there.

I don't know where to direct all this negative energy I've built up. I want to scream or break something, but none of it would help.

I don't want to face my thoughts.

I sigh and grab a book off the pile of favorites on my desk. I should probably read one of the new ones, but my mind isn't up to doing more than taking in the words I already know.

I open the book and immediately regret the decision. Tears start to well up as I read my mother's handwriting. *"For my Little Elle. Love you, Mom."* Running my fingers over the words, I feel the guilt weigh heavier on my chest.

I close the book and set it back on the pile. I try to stop the sobs I know are coming, but they make a quick return. Nothing is held back. I miss Mom. I miss Lilah. I miss when things felt normal. Or kinda mostly normal, anyway.

I should be doing everything I can to get better and

instead I'm lying here being angry over things I can't control.

Lilah can't do anything ever again and Mom can't do anything until she wakes up and I should be doing things because I can, and here I am doing nothing but wallowing.

Like a giant, useless, waste of survival.

The smell of something familiar baking in the kitchen slithers into the room, making my tummy grumble like it's been without food for years, and pushing my wallows to the side. Not forgotten, but not my focus for the moment.

I swing my legs off the bed and stare at the walker. I should be doing everything I can to get better, right?

Anger fuels determination.

I stand up, ignoring the walker, and use my desk as leverage to get me to the wall. I slowly walk down the hall and into the kitchen, using the wall for support along the way. Dylan looks up as I enter.

"Look at you, sans walker and everything." She smiles. "You sure you're good without it already?"

"I have the walls to help me." I can tell she's concerned, but she doesn't say anything else about it. I sit down at one of the barstools around the island counter. "What are you making?"

"Banana nut muffins. It was in your mama's recipe

book and looked like it had seen some use, so I went with it. Good choice?"

Nodding, I say, "Very good choice."

"Tough days need dessert." Dylan opens the oven and pulls out the muffins. She carefully picks one out of the pan and sets it in front of me. "Sumbitch is hot, so don't eat it just yet." She turns the oven off and grabs a plate to put the rest of them on.

Tough days need dessert. She always manages to pick up on my moods.

Dylan's phone vibrates, reminding me of Milo's text.

"Rob and Martha chose a day for the auction." I start picking at the muffin, taking little bites since it's still hot.

"Oh, they did?" Dylan asks, picking up a muffin for herself. "When is it?"

"Saturday."

She stops taking a bite. "This Saturday?"

I nod. "Mmhmm."

"That's awful soon."

"Yeah, that's like them, though. Rob, especially." I shrug and take a giant bite from the muffin, realizing too late that it's still too hot. I try to suck in some air as I chew. "These are really good," I say after swallowing.

Dylan chuckles. "Thank your mama. It's her

recipe." She gestures to the cookbook on the counter. It's filled with handwritten recipes Mom has tried over the years. "Well, Saturday is fine. We won't miss it." She pauses a second before adding, "Did they just tell you 'bout that today?"

"Yeah, Rob had Milo text me."

A grin as wide as the kitchen crosses Dylan's face. "Milo, huh? He got your number now?"

My eyes couldn't roll back further if I tried. "Rob doesn't know how to text, so he had Milo do it."

"Uh-huh. Well, as much as I can believe that, I doubt *Milo* would've needed much of an excuse to text you." She emphasizes his name again, really enjoying her teasing.

"We don't even know each other." I snatch another muffin off the counter and do my best to ignore her giggles.

"Looks to me like he's trying to fix that."

I plan to fall in love at least twice.

Lilah's words pop into my head and a knot forms in my throat. I can hear her laugh as if she were right next to me, can practically hear her urging me to either take the chance or let her have it.

I close my eyes and see her smile, the one she hated that I miss so much.

Whatever anger was left turns to guilt and sadness.

"So, what've we got planned for the day, kiddo?" Dylan wipes down the counter and moves the dishes she dirtied to the sink.

Clearing my throat, I say, "Nothing today."

"We could go visit your mama? Take her a muffin."

"She can't eat a muffin."

"No, but you can eat one for her." She winks and holds out two of them.

I can't help but grin, even as I bite my cheek. I take the muffins from her. "Okay."

"You stay there, I'll get your walker and slips." Dylan hurries around the counter and down the hall to my room, returning with my walker and a pair of slippers. She sets it all in front of me. "Put those on and I'll get these muffins ready to go."

Everything is black and white, like one of those old movies Mom likes to watch. The only color is the vibrant red in the scarf that twists and twirls behind Lilah as she walks down the road ahead of me.

She stops as the wind shifts direction, blowing her scarf to the front.

My legs keep moving, not letting me stop alongside her. I look back, reaching toward Lilah, and yell out her name. But she only smiles and I can't stop moving forward.

The wind catches her scarf, scooping it from her neck and tangling it in my arms as I try to claw at the air behind me.

Her smile grows distant.

Lilah waves goodbye, and suddenly everything is red like the scarf.

I slowly open my eyes, taking in the darkness of my room.

I pull my phone off the charger and check the time. It's late.

There's always a heavy feeling in my chest after dreams like that, an emptiness that feels so full of its own emptiness. I don't know how else to describe the feeling.

I sit up and grab my walker.

Dylan is sitting on the couch, reading the newspaper while a show plays in the background. I sit down in the recliner and move my walker so I can extend the footrest. Dylan looks up from her paper. "Get a good nap in?"

"Sure." I don't feel like talking about my nightmare this time.

She tosses the remote over to me. "You drive, kiddo. I'll go get the popcorn." Dylan stands and heads to the kitchen, calling back as she goes, "What do you want to drink?"

"Surprise me," I say. Nothing sounds good.

Dylan returns and hands me a drink. "Iced tea. Sweet tea, and I mean sweet." I take a drink, instantly glad I left the decision in her hands. She grins. "Good stuff?"

"Yes, thank you." I take another long drink and Dylan chuckles.

Sweet tea has always been a favorite of mine. Mom adds a lot of sugar and Dylan's tastes about the same. Another thing they have in common.

"You pick what we're watching. Popcorn is cookin' and I've got my paper if I don't like your choice." She winks at me before heading back to the kitchen.

Maybe I should keep a list of all the good things Dylan has been doing for me? Something to show Mom when she wakes up. Something that might help her not hold onto all that hate...

"Find anything good?" Dylan hands me a bag of popcorn and sits back on the couch with one of her own. I don't say anything and she asks, "You okay, kiddo?" She looks from me to the tv and back, probably noticing that I haven't touched the remote since she tossed it to me.

"I'm fine. Just... nightmares again. I don't want to think about it."

"Say no more. Let's take our mind off it." She picks up her newspaper and leaves it at that.

I force a smile and start flipping through the movie options, thankful that Dylan is good at knowing when to leave buttons unpressed.

I've never been much of a television fan. But I flip through until I find something I recognize and internally thank the streaming service for having it. Dylan nods and says, "Good choice," but she doesn't put her newspaper down.

It feels odd, but I let myself enjoy the movie. I laugh at the funny parts and push back the guilt for enjoying myself. I can dwell on it later. The moment feels good and I hold onto that feeling.

Even if I know it won't last.

Eight

Saturday comes faster than expected.

Rob and Martha rented out the local banquet hall to set up the silent auction, and word spread about the event fast. The place is packed.

All of the old overstock books from the back of the store have been packed into several "blind bags" and set out with labels indicating a theme for that bundle. It looks like several people–likely friends of Rob–and local businesses have been kind enough to donate other items, too.

It's overwhelming seeing what the community has put together for me and my family. Seeing so many people adding their bids to the lists in front of the auction items–bids that I'm sure are more than what the items are really worth–it's very humbling. Most of these people don't even know me, but they've shown up to do what they can.

Sometimes humanity wins out.

"See anything you want, kiddo?" Dylan eyes a mini fridge donated by one of the local businesses.

"Wouldn't it look bad to bid on something at an auction put together for me?"

She waves the notion away. "Nah, especially not if I'm the one doing the bidding."

A smile tugs the corner of my mouth. "I'm not going to stop you."

Dylan grins and says, "I'll be right back. Why don't you claim this table while I'm over there?" She gestures to the table in front of us and makes a beeline for the mini-fridge. I move closer to it but don't sit down just yet.

As thankful as I am for everyone being here and helping out, I'm uncomfortable being the center of attention. Most people are smiling and laughing together and having a great time doing a good thing for a broken girl. But I can see the sneaky glances that aren't quite so sneaky. I can feel the tension as their laughter fades when they see me and remember why they're really here.

I grip my walker, a knot forming in my chest.

Rob's laugh pulls my own attention across the

room. He's chatting up a group of people looking at one of the blind bags. He sees me and waves before continuing his conversation. He gestures in my direction and all eyes turn to me, eyes that immediately convey a mixture of innocent pity and sadness. *That's the girl with the walker we're raising money for tonight. The one who lost her best friend and whose mom is in a coma. The one that survived when she really shouldn't have. Yeah, that's her right there.*

The eyes shift back to the blind bag and it's obvious that Rob is really throwing some charisma into the auction. I may not be enjoying the moment, but I appreciate the care he's putting into this event. And the distraction he offers people attending.

I finally take a seat at the table, pulling my walker close to my chair so it's out of the way. Dylan is still at the auction table, watching a couple write their own bid for the mini-fridge. She waits a second after they walk away before sliding back over and writing another bid of her own. I wonder how long she plans to keep this up.

There's movement to my left and I turn to see who. It's the boy who doesn't stare, a big grin plastered to his face.

"Glad to see you made it," he says.

It seems silly to me that he might actually think I

wouldn't show up to a benefit auction in my honor, but I assume he's really just trying to open up conversation. "Of course."

"Rob and Martha really got this up and going, didn't they?" He looks around the room, taking in the size of the crowd.

"Rob always has a way of reaching people," I say.

"He really does." There's a moment of awkward silence that seems to affect me more than him. "So, how are you doing? Like, with your healing and all?" His voice is softer, but doesn't hold that sour drip of pity most people can't hide.

"Better everyday." I gesture to the walker sitting next to me, not wanting it to be an elephant in our conversation.

He nods. "I had to do physical therapy when I was a kid. It's tough, but it's amazing how much it helps. I can't even imagine going through it over something like you are."

It doesn't phase him, just like when we first met and he never once stared at my wheelchair.

I wonder what made him have to go through physical therapy. A car accident like mine? A sports injury? A random unavoidable event? Is that why he treats me so normal?

I wonder for a moment if my curiosity is as bad as the stares I hate so much.

"So have you read that book yet?" His grin widens as he asks the question. It's easy to see he's genuinely excited to hear my answer.

The stack of new books left untouched next to my bed comes to mind. "Not yet, but I will." I don't know why I said "I will" like it's going to happen tonight or something.

"You have to text me when you do. There are so many good poems in there." Milo glances down, probably trying to hide the light shade of red spreading across his cheeks as he blurts out, "Do you mind if I text you? I mean, I know I already did when Rob asked me to, and then when I asked how you were, but–" He sucks in a deep breath and stops talking, the red on his face turning even brighter.

"Sure." The word comes out before I even think about it. Do I really want him to text me? Where on Earth is my mind right now?

I can feel Dylan watching me with Milo. I glance over and she's not hiding her amusement. I know that grin. It's the same one she always gets when she teases me.

Great. I know I'll have that to look forward to later.

Milo follows my gaze and says, "Oh, hey, isn't that your home nurse? I remember seeing her with you at the bookstore."

"She's my aunt." I'm quick to say it, realizing just as fast that it's the first time I've really referred to her as such. Part of me feels guilty, knowing Mom won't like that. But I'm really growing to see Dylan as the family she is more and more every day.

"Oh, cool," he says. "She looks happy about something."

"Yeah, I'm sure she is." Milo looks a little confused, but I don't offer anything to let him in on the joke. "I should probably go see how her bid is going, actually." I grab the opportunity to flee.

Disappointment crosses his face so fast I'm not sure I really saw it. "Yeah, I'm sure Rob has something he needs me to do around here anyway." He awkwardly fumbles his hands into his pockets. "It was nice talking to you, Ellessy."

The way he said my name was nice. "Yeah, you too." I hope I'm not the one blushing this time.

Milo gives a short wave and wanders off toward Rob. I watch him for a second before I head over to Dylan. Knowing her, I'm sure she already has jokes ready.

Dylan meets me halfway. "Saw you talkin' to your boy."

I can feel the heat rise in my cheeks for sure. "It's nothing."

She raises an eyebrow. "Do you not see that boy has a crush on you?"

"He can have a crush if he wants to; it's not my business." I'm a little more defensive than I mean to be.

Dylan presses on. "And you don't think he's cute?"

I look over at him. He's laughing along with Rob as they talk up more people considering the auction items. His laugh is loud and higher pitched than expected. He laughs with his whole face, like he's not afraid to look silly over a good joke.

I shrug. "He's cute."

"Uh-huh. And you like him?" Dylan's smile could crack her face.

But a weight creeps over my shoulders. "I don't know."

Something in me feels guilty at the idea of liking him as anything more than a friend. Lilah is dead and I'm not. Mom is in a coma and I'm here at what's basically a party in my favor. Why should I think for even a second that it's okay for me to be interested in a cute boy when they can't even stand up and tell me how they feel about it? How is that fair to them?

If love wasn't part of the plans before, why should I entertain the idea of a crush now?

"Hey, you okay, kiddo?" Dylan's voice is soft. "You need to get out of here? We can go home if you want. No one is gonna think anything of it, Elle."

I consider her offer for only a moment before shaking my head. "No, we should stay."

"Are you sure?" Her concern warms my heart.

I think I'm going to have to beg Mom to let her stay.

"Yeah." I give Dylan a weak smile, hoping it's convincing enough to ease her concern.

She looks me over a bit, probably trying to decide if she should make the decision for me. "Alright," she says. "But you tell me when you're ready. I'll have us out of here and halfway to onion rings before anyone realizes we're gone."

"You better go check on your mini-fridge." I change the subject, gesturing to the couple writing in their bid now.

"Nah, I can hang out with you. Mini-fridge ain't that important."

"Go." I give her a light push. "I wouldn't mind a few minutes to myself anyway."

Dylan hesitates. "Okay, but don't run off." She winks and adds, "I can see you over there, so just wave me over if you need me." She squeezes my shoulder again before running off to secure her hold on the fridge.

I look around, making sure no one is heading my way, then go back to my seat at the table and close my eyes. One, two, three, four, five; I breathe in. One, two, three, four, five; I let it out. I know I'm supposed to hold the breath in, but that part always makes me dizzy. Dylan says this is supposed to help you relax. I don't know if it really does, but it can't hurt to try, right?

Because right now, I don't really feel like being here, and I didn't want to admit that to her. I don't want to leave early and get those pity stares, or for people to tell us "they understand" when they really don't.

My mind spins a thousand things they might think if we leave now.

She's the girl we're here for, the one who survived the car accident. She's probably tired from the brain damage–probably needs some meds and a nap. It's okay if she goes home, she probably doesn't want to think about all this, anyway. I really feel so sorry for the girl, you know?

Things that aren't really mean or wrong of anyone to think, but that I'd rather not encourage.

I focus on my breathing, on keeping my mind distracted.

The rest of the auction goes by in a blur. Dylan brings me some food from the concession stand and we eat. People I know and more that I don't come around to speak to me, telling me how happy they are to see me looking so well and how sorry they are that I had to experience something so tragic so young. They wish me the best and go back to laughing over small talk with the rest of the crowd.

Dylan stays with me, only leaving when someone stops by the mini-fridge and coming back after she writes in a higher number.

Rob announces the last call for bids and there's a sudden flurry of activity around the tables, Dylan among them, before everyone gets settled in their seats.

Rob returns to the podium and says, "Alright, everyone. Martha is going around to collect all of the cards." He gestures to her near one of the tables and she gives a wave with a hand that's full of auction cards. "Now, you've got time to grab some dessert if you haven't already while we're gathering up the bids–I suggest some of Ruthie's homemade caramel apple pie while there's still some left–and then we'll get this benefit auction underway and start announcing some winners!"

Murmurs rustle through the crowd as some people wander to the concession stand and others find a seat facing the podium. It isn't long before Martha hands the cards off to Rob, and everyone takes it as a cue to get settled and stop talking.

It takes a while to read off all the winning bids. I didn't realize just how many items were up for auction until now. My heart swells over how many people in the community really did what they could to help someone they don't even really know. Tears well up in my eyes and Dylan throws her arm around me. "That's all for you and yours, kiddo." She squeezes me close.

Dylan also gets her mini-fridge, throwing up her fist at the sound of her name. The crowd chuckles. I cover my face.

Rob wraps everything up with one last bit of speech. "Thank you to everyone for coming out and offering your things and your money for the cause. We're here to help one of our own at Rob and Martha's, Miss Ellessy Porter." He waves a hand to me with a warm smile. He gives the crowd a moment to clap and they embrace it. "Ellessy has worked at our bookstore for three years now, and she and her mother are some of the kindest people you could ever ask to meet. I know, from the very top to the bottom of my heart, that Ellessy and her mother are so appreciative of what we're doing for them here tonight. Elle is a strong, young woman, and we're so thankful she's still here with us. Her mama still has a healing journey ahead of her, and may we all continue to keep both of them in our prayers. Thanks again and stay safe."

Rob gives a final wave and Martha steps up to the podium to add, "Everyone who had a winning bid, follow us over to the table by the entrance, and we'll get things settled."

Dylan wipes a tear from my face, pulling me out of the moment. "You ready to head home now, kiddo?"

My lip trembles as I tell her, "Yes." I can feel that familiar pressure building up in my chest. I don't want to be here anymore.

"Let's get you out to the SUV and I'll take care of my bid, sound good?"

I nod, too overwhelmed to say anything in return.

Dylan goes into Mama Bear Mode. She maneuvers me through the crowd, saying what needs to be said to avoid conversation. *Thank you. She's thankful. She's tired. We appreciate everything. We'll talk to you later. She needs to get home. Thanks, so much.*

They all make room for the girl with the walker, and we're out of there in no time.

"I'll tell Rob and Martha you needed to get home and all that, kiddo. Just get buckled in and relax for a minute." Dylan puts my walker in the back and rushes inside to finish things up.

I let my head sink into the headrest, closing my eyes, trying to ignore the intrusive thoughts filling the silence in my mind.

My pocket vibrates. I pull out my phone, expecting to see a text from Dylan, and see one from Milo instead.

> It was nice talking to you today. :)

It buzzes again.

> Hope you get some rest.

I put my phone back in my pocket and close my eyes again.

The back door opening tells me Dylan is back. She grunts as she slides the mini-fridge into the SUV. Then she closes the door and comes around to get in the driver's seat. "You want those onion rings?"

Tears well up again as I look at her and nod.

She strokes my cheek and gives me a quiet look that

says everything. Without a word, she turns the key and we leave.

Nine

Two months. Two months and one week if you count the time I spent in the hospital. That's how long it has taken me to get to this point.

Mom still isn't awake, but today is my last physical therapy session with Louis and I'm officially not using the walker anymore. Yeah, I've got a very noticeable limp and I don't think I'll be running any time soon, but I'm walking on my own. I don't have to be the "Girl with the Walker" anymore.

No more stares from strangers.

Or not as many stares, anyway. My limp isn't hiding and my left foot feels like there's concrete in it, so it hits the ground harder than my right foot.

Walking kind of sounds like I can't decide if I want to stomp or not. But I've been dealing with that all ready while using the walker, so it's nothing new.

"Alright, Ellessy, I want you to do the penguin game again." Louis pulls the game up on the TV as I step onto the connected balance board we've been using lately. He's made it clear he doesn't think I'm ready to be done with therapy. "I really want to work on your balance as much as possible today."

Louis didn't seem very happy when he learned that this was my final session with him. I'm honestly not sure what factors played into this being the last one. I'm assuming it's mainly my insurance, but I haven't asked. There isn't anything I can do about it anyway.

"You don't think I'm ready, do you?" I ask him, more determined to prove that I am.

I need to be. Mom could wake up any day. And, while I still plan to see if Dylan can stay, I want to be able to help take care of Mom when she gets home.

Other than the crease in his brow, Louis' face doesn't give much away. "I think you can do anything you push yourself to do. My worry is that you're pushing yourself too much, too fast." He stands ready to hold me steady if I start to fall. "It hasn't been that long since you were still mostly wheelchair dependent during our sessions."

"I'm still surprised we're already off the walker," Dylan chimes in over her magazine. She's sitting in a chair nearby, facing us.

Louis nods. "Your progress has been nothing short of spectacular, Ellessy. You've really been working hard here and it has clearly paid off. But, I do feel like even just a couple more sessions would do you good, especially with this being your first one leaving without the walker."

"They wouldn't let me stop if they thought it was too soon, would they?" I ask.

Their silence sends a cold wave down my spine.

"That's a tricky topic," Louis finally says. I whip my head around to look at him, throwing my balance off. He's quick to help me reposition myself and adds, "You've shown me time and again how determined you are. You'll be fine."

"But you just said I need a couple more sessions." I try to focus on the game, but it's difficult with the bubble of pressure suddenly building in my chest.

"I would like for you to have a few more, yes. But, I know you'll be fine, Ellessy. You've proven as much already."

The pressure doesn't go away, but his assurance eases it just a little.

"It's just how the system works, kiddo," Dylan

says, adding, "But you've got me to keep things going at home. Hell, we can even get one of these game doo-dats for the house, if you want!"

I glare at her. "I think this is the one part of physical therapy that I won't miss at all."

Dylan and Louis both laugh. They know how much I've grown to hate this thing. I've never been a gamer, anyway, but I truly can't understand how people play this for fun.

We work on my balance until the last fifteen minutes of the session, spending that time using the exercise bands, which I much prefer. Louis pushes me to my limits and I wonder if he's trying to make up for the time we won't have. He should give himself more credit. I'd still be in the wheelchair if it weren't for the work he's done with me.

"Alright, Ellessy. I'd say that's a wrap." He stands with his arms crossed.

"Already?" I set the exercise band to the side and slip my shoes back on.

"Indeed. Do you feel good about everything you've accomplished?"

"I think if Mom were awake right now, she'd be really proud." I'm not sure why I say it, but a lump forms in my throat as soon as the words are out.

"Damn right she would be," Dylan says.

Louis slowly nods as a grin hits his face. "I agree. Honestly, I think you're ready for anything. Maybe not video games, but..." I roll my eyes as Dylan snorts. "Really, though. Your Mom *is* going to be proud when she learns how hard you worked here."

"He's right as rain clouds in April, Elle." Dylan sets her magazine aside. "And you know darn well we're proud of you, too."

"Absolutely," Louis says.

"Thanks." I smile and add, "No wheelchair, no walker, and I can wiggle my toes."

"I'd call that a win." Louis holds out his hand and firmly shakes mine. "Well, Ellessy, you take care. I do not want to see you back in here for anything else." He winks and turns to shake Dylan's hand, as well.

"Oh no, no more extracurricular danger for this one, I'll see to that." Dylan laughs loud enough to pull the eyes of everyone in the large room. As usual, she either doesn't notice or doesn't care.

"You know I'll hold you to it." Louis points at her, a grin big enough to match her energy across his face.

"Maybe if Mom needs physical therapy, I'll see you again?" I ask.

"So long as that's the only reason I see you walking back in here, okay?"

I smile. "Okay."

"You hear that? *Walking* back in here," Dylan says, making a walking gesture with her fingers. She gives another loud laugh before adding, "Alright, kiddo, let's ditch this place before they kick me out for being too much of a riot."

Dylan follows me out to the SUV and I get in without her help.

Maybe when Mom wakes up we can bring her out to meet Louis sometime? If she needs physical therapy, maybe he'll be her therapist? As much as I hope she doesn't need it, the idea makes me smile.

"So how does it feel graduatin' physical therapy?" Dylan reaches over and gives my knee a playful tap. "Ready to hike Everest?" She snorts at her joke. It always cracks me up how much Dylan cracks herself up.

"I know I'm not back to normal, but it feels good to be where I'm at."

Dylan shakes her head. "Nobody gets back to normal, kiddo. You get a new normal and you learn to live with it." It's obvious she's seen this as a nurse. "But the more you walk on it, the closer it'll get to how it was. You don't need physical therapy for that. Hell, that's what you've got me for! We can get up early and go walking every mornin'!" She glances at me with a grin.

"Don't you dare wake me up early for a walk, Dylan."

She laughs some more and says, "Nah, I wouldn't do that, don't worry. We can plan some trips to the mall or somethin'. Walk around and window shop. You kids still like to do that?"

It actually does sound like a nice idea. Especially now that people staring isn't as big of a worry. "Maybe Mom could walk with us, too? When she wakes up."

"Definitely." She smiles, but I can see some sadness behind it. I don't know if it's because she knows she'll have to leave when Mom wakes up, or if she's worried about how long it'll be before that happens. I don't ask.

I feel my phone vibrate and pull it out to check the notification. It's a text from Milo.

> Hey, Rob wants you to stop by when you get a chance. He has the donations from the auction ready for you.

"That your boy?" Dylan has the grin I've come to expect.

I ignore her teasing. "Rob wants us to stop by the bookstore."

We've already passed it, so Dylan gets in the left lane to turn around and head back.

"Auction stuff?" she asks.

I nod and reply to the text.

> We're on the way.

"Yeah, he said the donations are ready." I'm not sure what all had to be done before the money could be handed over to us, but it didn't seem to take as long as I expected. Not that I have much reference for this stuff anyway.

"Tell him we'll be there pretty quick."

"I did." I look at the time on the radio and add, "The store doesn't close for a few more hours, anyway."

"Better to not make them wait on something like this," Dylan says. "Besides, I know you were wanting to talk to Rob about coming back to work after therapy was done."

I did mention I was hoping to get back to work again soon. I'm probably still a few weeks away from being ready, but it might be a good idea to let Rob know I'm thinking about it. Just a couple hours a week would be nice, until I'm able to do more. Knowing Rob and Martha, they'll be able to make something work.

We pull up a few moments later. Out of habit, Dylan runs around to help me out of the SUV. "I've got it," I say.

She grins. "By golly, you do."

It's nice being able to do these things by myself again.

The door to the shop opens before we get to it. Martha welcomes us in with a warm smile. "How are you doing today, Elle?" she asks, pulling me into an embrace as warm as her smile.

"I'm good," I say, still feeling the excitement from therapy.

Martha gently takes my face in her hands. "You look tired!"

"Physical therapy day. Our last appointment," Dylan says.

Martha turns to look at her. "Oh that's wonderful. Onward on the path to healing!" She smiles and claps her hands together. "Now... Dylan?" She asks it. Martha's never been good with names, probably why Rob tends to do all the talking.

Dylan nods, clearly unbothered, "Yeah, that's me."

Martha smiles, looking relieved that her memory didn't fail her this time. "Right. If you want to follow me, Rob has everything ready back in the office. This way." She turns and starts walking toward the door at the back of the store.

"You comin', kiddo?" Dylan asks. "This is all for you and your mama, after all."

I start to nod, but something catches my eye behind her. Milo sidles over to us. For the first time, the boy who doesn't stare is staring. "Your walker is gone!"

Dylan's eyes bounce between the two of us as she waits for my response.

"You go. I don't want to push myself too hard today."

"Mmhmm." She pauses a second longer before walking to the door Martha is patiently holding open for her.

"I can go get you a chair if you need one," Milo offers.

I shake my head. "I'll be fine. I don't think we'll be here long anyway."

"Okay. Let me know if you change your mind, though. I don't at all mind running back to grab you one." He pumps his arms like he would if he were running.

"Thank you. I'm okay, though." I can't stop my smile.

There's an awkward silence between us as he looks

at his feet. His dark, messy hair hangs down in the front, hiding the blush I can only guess he's sporting right now.

"So, uh..." he runs a hand through his hair as he looks back up at me. Clearing his throat, he continues, "How have you been?" He shoves his hands in his pockets, but doesn't try to hide the scarlet spreading across his cheeks this time.

"I've been okay." *As okay as I can be*. "How about you?"

"I've been good."

The uncomfortable silence starts to settle again. "I was thinking about asking Rob if I could come back to work soon."

Milo perks up. "Really?"

I repeat my plan to him. "Yeah, just for a few hours here and there. Until I can do more, you know?"

"Yeah, definitely. That's awesome." His smile fades. "Rob isn't here, though."

The shop may be called "Rob and Martha's," but Rob is the one who runs it. Martha doesn't like to mess with that side of the business. "Will he be coming back in?"

Milo shakes his head. "Not until tomorrow."

The door to the back opens and Dylan returns. I

can tell she's ready to tease me, so I quickly ask her, "Did you get everything we needed?"

She holds up a manilla envelope. "All here."

"Rob isn't here today so we have to come back tomorrow."

"Can do, kiddo." She comes to a stop next to us. "Anything else you need to do while we're here?"

I shake my head. "No."

"Well, you heard her," she says to Milo. "I'd say it's time for us to go." She slaps him on the back and he stumbles forward a step.

"Let me get the door for you," he says, rushing over to hold the door open.

Dylan thanks him for both of us as we walk out. We get into the SUV, and I glance at the shop. Milo waves at us as we pull away.

"I'm thinking waffles for a late lunch. That sound good?" Dylan asks. I'm surprised she's not pushing for details about what Milo and I talked about, but I don't give her a reason to go there. Instead, my stomach grumbles. She laughs and says, "Sounds like a 'yes' to me."

I need a nap, but I can't sleep. My mind keeps thinking of the things I don't want to think about–of all the what ifs that might have made things different.

What if we hadn't chosen that restaurant to go to? What if I had let Lilah sit in the front? What if I had tried talking mom into letting me drive instead of her?

Would we all be fine? Would it be Lilah here and not me? Would I be in a coma and not Mom?

Would we all be gone?

What if we had left the house just a few minutes later? A few minutes earlier? What if we had taken a different road? One that didn't have that semi on it?

My heart lurches as I bolt upright in bed, suddenly realizing that I've never once stopped to think about the person driving that truck.

I grab my phone and search "car accident" and the date, hoping to find an article about it online. A few options pop up immediately, and I go to the first article listed.

"Woman, Two Teens, Truck Driver Involved in Rook County Car Accident – Two Fatalities"

My heart sinks even further as I continue reading the article. His name was William Wright. He was only 52.

I go back and pull up the next article. This one was posted a few days ago. It says he likely had a heart attack at the wheel, causing him to lose control and strike Mom's car.

I go back again and type in "William Wright obituary." The top link is an ad for a funeral home, but the second one is a newspaper link.

I read his obituary. Then I read it again. I read it so many times, I almost memorize it.

William "Bill" Wright. 52. From Iowa. Divorced. One child; a son aged 33.

I wonder what his family must be going through, if they are struggling with the same questions as me. Do they cycle through the what ifs like I do? Do they try to imagine what could have been done to change what happened that day? Are they kept awake by the questions we can never answer?

Do they blame themselves?

Do they blame me?

I wipe the pain from my face and take a long, deep breath. As much as I need a nap, I don't think it's happening at this point.

I want my mom.

Sliding my slippers on, I get up and walk to the living room. Dylan glances up from her book as I enter. "I want to go see Mom." The emotion is thick in my voice.

She doesn't hesitate. Dylan dog-ears her book and sets it on the end table. "Let's go see your mom."

Neither of us say anything on the car ride. Dylan doesn't even listen to her old music. I swear she has a sixth sense when it comes to picking up on other people's emotions. Maybe it's a nurse thing. Maybe it's a Dylan thing. I'm thankful, either way.

Mom is still in the same room, hooked up to the same machines, looking more like Mom than she did the first time I saw her in here. But still looking like a broken, sleeping princess all the same.

But she's here. She's alive and I see her here and know that she'll be home again eventually.

Not like Lilah.

Not like William Wright.

I can still hold her hand and play with her hair. I can kiss her forehead and see her chest rise and fall as she breathes, even if it's not really her doing the breathing yet.

I can feel her warmth and know that any day, she is going to wake up and be my mom again.

I didn't realize how much I was holding in, but it all comes bursting out like a water balloon smacking against the pavement.

I need her. I need my mom.

Seeing her like this turns a knife in my gut, and I don't have anymore room for the pain.

I hold her hand and cry. I tell her I love her and miss her, and how much I need her to wake up.

I cry until Dylan comes in and tells me her nurses need to turn her. I cry as we leave the hospital, and the entire ride home. I cry until I crawl into bed and exhaust myself to sleep.

And then I dream about dead strangers in semis and cry there, too.

Ten

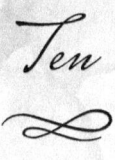

The auction raised quite a bit of money, and Martha and Dylan took care of everything behind the scenes. What we took home was more than enough to keep the bills paid and the cabinets full for a while. That's even after sending quite a bit of the earnings to Lilah's family. I insisted, but it's not like there was much protest.

Dylan says Mom will likely need a lot of things her insurance might not cover when she wakes up. She says that everyone is different, but she's seen some patients wake up from comas and have to learn to use their entire body again.

I know how hard it was for me with just my leg. I really hope Mom doesn't have to go through that with her whole body.

Without knowing what Mom might need when she wakes up, Dylan and I agree it's best to put the majority of the money into savings.

"We should put it in the savings account my college fund is in since we're already using it anyway."

Dylan isn't thrilled. "You don't have to do that, kiddo."

"I don't even know if I'm going anymore," I say. She grumbles, but keeps whatever argument she has to herself. "And I really don't want you using your money on me any more than you already have."

I know she wants to do more, but I also know she's still paying bills at her place in Illinois while she's here helping me. She sighs, obviously irritated at the situation. "Alright, Elle. Grab your purse, let's go."

I throw on my shoes and grab my things. The only plans for today are to take care of the donation money and stop by the bookstore to talk to Rob.

I'm ready to start checking them off the list.

It's pretty simple when we get to the bank. I transfer my college fund to checking, and move the auction donations to take its place in my savings account. I don't know if this is how you "adult" or not, but I'd say it's a step in the right direction.

We push things along as fast as we can. The clerk

mentions being at the auction and tells us how sorry she is that I went through such a thing so young, how inspiring it is to see me still going after everything. I shift uncomfortably as she tells us how she bid on one of the mystery bundles and won, but hasn't opened it yet.

I honestly just didn't know how to respond.

Dylan does it for me, thanking her and turning to leave before the clerk can do anything more than wish us a great day.

"Goodness that woman could write a story for a stranger, couldn't she?" Dylan says as we climb into the SUV. She shakes her head and starts the vehicle. "You want anything before we head to the book shop? Onion rings or anything?"

"No, thank you."

Dylan gapes at me. "Did I hear that right? You just turned down onion rings?"

I giggle and shrug. "They just don't sound good anymore."

"Well I never thought I'd see the day." Dylan does her best to be overdramatic.

"Sweet tea sounds good, though." Ever since she made that one for me the other night, I've been craving it.

She laughs. "You're speaking the language of my

heart now." Nudging my shoulder with hers she adds, "I can always go for one of those."

We drive to the fast food place across from the bookstore. I've had their sweet tea before and know it's good.

Dylan pulls up and tells the drive-through speaker our order.

I go to grab my wallet and Dylan smacks my hand. "None of that," she says. "I'm payin'."

I roll my eyes. "You have to let me pay sometime, you know."

Dylan snorts. "Yeah, we'll see about that."

She pays the lady at the first window, but the line doesn't move.

"So we're seeing about you comin' back to work?" Dylan asks, impatiently tapping her fingers on the steering wheel.

"Yes. I'm hoping I can come in tomorrow for a few hours."

"Yeah, I think that would be good for you. A little to start with. Build you up until you can go back to what you're used to." Dylan smacks the wheel and says, "Come on! Did you order for the whole family?"

"Have you ever heard the term 'hangry'?" I ask, trying to hold back my laughter.

"I'm not that old," she says, side-eyeing me.

"Well I think you've got that. But for drinks. Like, 'thangry' or something."

Dylan chuckles, finally pulling up to the second window for our teas. "Worsty?" she offers, as she takes the drinks. The kid handing them to her loses their smile and gives Dylan a funny look.

"How about 'dehirated'?" I offer. She furrows her brows, so I explain, "Dehydrated and irate."

She laughs. "I like that one. It doesn't roll off the tongue like 'hangry', but it'll do."

Dylan passes me my drink and pulls out of the drive-through, crossing the street to Rob and Martha's.

Abbie's car is parked out front. She's the other woman who works here besides me, Rob, and Martha. And Milo, now, too. She's a nice woman and I really enjoy working with her. She's in her thirties, but you wouldn't know it by looking at her.

We walk in and she greets us at the door, throwing out her arms and pulling me into a hug. "Oh, it's so good to see you, Ellie," she says. Abbie is the only person who calls me that. I don't think the nickname suits me, but I don't mind. It sounds right coming from her.

"Hey, Abbie," I say.

"How are you? I saw you at the auction, but never had a chance to get away and say 'hi' to you."

"You were at the auction?" I ask.

"Yeah, I was back in the concession, so I'm sure you didn't see me." She pulls back and takes a good look at me. She has a sad smile, but I feel the warmth her eyes carry. "You look good, Ellie." She turns to Dylan and adds, "You've done a great job taking care of her."

I look at the two of them, confused. They seem like they know each other, but they've never met. Dylan catches my look and asks, "You don't remember her coming by the house, do you?"

Alarm shoots through my body as I search my mind for the memory. I haven't seen Abbie since before my accident. I'm sure of it.

"I stopped by a few days after you got home," Abbie says. "Just to see how you were doing and drop off some food."

Another wave shoots through me, sending a cold chill down my spine and up into the back of my skull. I can't remember her being there but I can still feel how the water from the shower hit me on my first night home. How can I remember one and not the other?

"How long were you there?" Maybe she only stopped by for a few minutes and I barely saw her?

"Oh, she stopped in for a few hours, I'd say," Dylan says, looking to Abbie for confirmation. She nods as

Dylan continues, "Talked to you for about twenty minutes before you went down for another nap, and then stayed a while more and talked with me."

My stomach drops. Twenty more minutes of my life added to the rest of the moments I've lost. I know memory problems are supposed to be common with traumatic brain injuries, but I had thought maybe I was lucky.

"I don't remember..." I say, embarrassed to admit it.

"Oh, that's okay, Ellie. It's nothing to worry about," Abbie says. Her warm smile makes me feel a tiny bit better.

"Don't sweat it, kiddo," Dylan adds. "That's normal with a TBI. You're probably gonna realize there's a lot of things you don't remember." She squeezes my shoulder and winks. "That's what you've got me for."

Abbie effortlessly moves the conversation on. "So what brings you in today?"

"I, uh," I shake my head, trying to pull myself away from this new information. "I wanted to ask Rob about letting me come back to work. I was told he should be in today."

"I think I'm boring her at the house," Dylan says.

Abbie laughs. "I think that would be great for you,

Ellie." She gestures to the door at the back of the store. "Rob's in the office."

"Thanks," I say, turning to look at Dylan.

"You go on, I'm gonna visit with Ms. Abbie," she tells me.

I pause a moment before turning toward the back of the store, my mind still halted on the memory thing. How much else is there that I've lost? What moments have slipped from my memory without me having a clue? How many situations like this have I already been in and don't remember?

I don't know how to fix this or if I even can, but I add it to my plans. How can I take care of myself when Dylan leaves–if she has to–if I'm not even sure I'll remember what I've already done?

I step into the back and head down the tiny hall to the left. The office is at the end, a small room with a homey vibe. The door is already open when I get to it. I think Rob would just remove the door if Martha would let him.

Rob is seated at the desk in the center of the room, but stands the moment he sees me. "Ellessy! It's great to see you in today." He always makes me feel like I'm speaking with family. As long as I've known him, both from working here and being a regular customer before, he and Martha basically *are* my second family.

"What brings you in?" He pulls a chair around for me and leans against his desk.

"I wanted to talk to you about coming back to work." I settle into the seat, a nice puff of dust hissing out as I do. Clearly, most of the talking here tends to occur on the sales floor.

Rob's eyebrows fly up. "You're ready to come back?"

"Not full time or anything. Maybe a few hours a week at first?" I've practiced this conversation so many times in my head.

He bites the inside of his cheek while he thinks about it, slowly nodding as he moves around the desk to sit behind it again. "If you think you're ready, then I think we can put you on a shift with Milo or Abbie for a bit," he says, quickly adding, "Just to start. Not that we don't believe in you! We don't want you to push yourself."

"Thank you." I take a deep breath, feeling a lot of my worry ease away. One step closer to being back to normal.

Rob smiles. "When were you wanting to start?"

"I'm free tomorrow." Zero hesitation.

He shifts some things around on his desk so that the schedule is in front of him. "Milo has the floor tomorrow. You can come in anytime you're ready. I'll tell him to be expecting you." Rob stands again and comes around to shake my hand. "It's really great to see you coming along so well, Ellessy. We'll be glad to have you back. I know we've had a lot of customers asking about you, so they'll be happy to see you back in the shop again."

He gives my hand a firm shake, warmth emanating from his heart directly into it.

"I'm happy to be coming back."

Rob walks with me back to the sales floor. We can hear Dylan's laughter before we even get to the door. She and Abbie are in a fit of giggles, standing where I left them.

"Well, what joke were we ten feet late for?" Rob asks, reaching out to shake Dylan's hand.

"Oh, it's nothing," Abbie says, her face flush from laughter. "Dylan was telling me some stories from her nursing days."

"Things got pretty crazy on the night shift," Dylan says with a wink.

"Oh? Well, maybe you should write a book about it sometime? Then we could have our own book signing and everything!" Rob gestures around the shop, obviously imagining such an event.

"You definitely should, Dylan," Abbie says. "I know I'd read it. Especially after *that* story." She snorts, blushing again. Something tells me it's a story I don't want to hear.

"No, sir, writing is not meant for me." She waves the notion away. "Two possums with half a nanner peel could do better, trust me."

"If you change your mind, my store better be the first to have your book on the shelves." Rob smiles and turns to walk back to the office, saying "book signing" in a singsong voice as he goes.

Dylan shakes her head and asks, "You get it figured out, kiddo?"

"Yeah, he said I can come in whenever I want tomorrow."

"Whenever?" she asks.

I nod. "I'll be working with Milo. Rob said he'll make sure he knows I'm coming in."

"Mmhmm." Dylan gives a side glance to Abbie. They both grin.

I internally roll my eyes. Maybe a little externally, too. "Well, it was good to see you, Abbie," I say, completely ignoring everything else.

She reaches out for another hug. "It is always good to see you, too, Ellie." Pulling away, she adds, "I'll try to stop by the house again sometime soon, if that's okay?"

I nod. "Yeah, that's fine."

"We'll see you soon, Abbie," Dylan says. She holds the front door open for me and I lead the way.

"Wanna grab another sweet tea before we head home?" I ask, wiggling my empty cup in front of me.

Dylan chuckles, showing me that hers is still half full. "Hop in, kiddo, we'll go get your new fix."

I smile, thankful she puts up with me.

Eleven

For once, I didn't have to face the nightmares. But, sleep also didn't come easy last night.

I've always liked my job, but I'm more excited to go to work than I've ever been before, to finally have a larger sense of normalcy back in my life.

"Do you want me to hang out at the shop with you today, or just come back around when you're ready to leave?" Dylan asks. She's trying her best to hide it, but I can tell she's as nervous for me as she is happy.

"I'll just text you," I tell her. "I don't know how long I'll end up staying, so I don't want you to be bored." I really want to do this on my own.

There's a sparkle in her eyes as she says, "Oh, I think there will be plenty of entertainment."

I roll my eyes. I know she's only teasing, but she's

really getting too much enjoyment out of the fact that Milo seems to like me. "I'm ready if you are."

Dylan sets the newspaper she was reading on the kitchen counter. "Let's scoot, then." She chugs the last of her coffee and sets the cup in the sink before turning to leave.

The light on the coffee maker is still glaring bright red. "Wait," I say, feeling that pressure in my chest again. Dylan pauses at the front door as I walk over and turn it off. The pressure eases but doesn't go away.

"You sure you want to go today?" she asks.

"Yeah, let's do it." She opens the door and I hurry past her before I can change my mind.

That feeling bugs me the entire ride to the shop, a gnawing that keeps me from. concentrating on anything else. I don't even realize Dylan swung by the drive-through for sweet tea until she's handing it to me.

"You sure you're alright, kiddo?" Her tone says she already knows something is bothering me.

"I'm fine." Honestly, I don't even know what the problem is. I just keep thinking about the coffee maker.

She nods and drives across the street to Rob and Martha's. She shuts the SUV off when she parks and places her hand on my knee. "You can always talk to me about anything, kiddo. I won't judge you. I won't ask questions if you don't want me to. But you can always talk to me, okay?"

I forget sometimes that we haven't known each other that long. Blood makes her my aunt, but I've grown to see her like a best–like a close friend.

A sharp pang of guilt hits my heart. *Lilah*. It doesn't feel right to call anyone else my best friend. No one could ever take her place.

Still, Dylan and I have grown pretty close. She's nothing like the person Mom thinks she is. And I know it's going to hurt everyone when Mom wakes up and I have to convince her of that.

"I love you, Dylan." It's all I can say. I reach across and pull her into a hug. She squeezes just a little too tight, but that's okay. Part of me feels like she's trying to squeeze some of my worries away, and I think I need that right now.

"Love you, too, Elle. Now go on and get to work." Dabbing at her eyes with the bottom of her shirt, she adds, "Don't want you late on your first day back."

I smile, wanting to tell her I can't be late when I was told to come in whenever I want, but I bite my tongue. "I'll text you when I'm ready."

It feels weird walking into the shop to work again.

It's been almost three months since I've clocked in. What if I've forgotten everything?

I suddenly want to barf.

"Hey!" Milo bounds over to me, full of energy. "Rob said you'd be in sometime today." His attitude is infectious. The feeling in my gut slips away.

"Hello, Milo." I realize I've never said his name out loud, not that I remember, anyway. The word feels weird tumbling out of my mouth.

"Hello, Ellessy," he says.

There's an awkward pause as he follows me to the back. Awkward for me, I guess. Milo seems oblivious to it as he stands in the doorway to the back hall.

"So, uh, what have you done on the big checklist so far?" I ask, writing my name and the time on the time sheet. Martha keeps a checklist of the major things outside of normal that needs to be done each day. She's super meticulous about it, without being overbearing. Rob may run things, but Martha keeps it running smoothly.

Milo's smile falters long enough for me to barely catch it. "Well... we've been really slow today... So, I sort of already got everything done." He looks like a cat with its paw in the fish bowl, something I realize Dylan would say. She must be rubbing off on me.

A slow grin spreads across my face. "*Everything* on

the list?" I walk past him, moving back into the front area of the store.

He follows. "Yeah, but there wasn't much that needed done today. We got caught up with everything when we were preparing for the auction." He shrugs and adds, "Martha was convinced we'd be super behind with all of that going on, so she had us work a few lists ahead and... well, now we're more caught up than we've ever been."

That sounds exactly like something Martha would do. Looking around, I ask, "So, what have you been working on?"

"Oh, I just finished with the task list, so nothing other than that. I was about to start walking the shelves and making sure everything is where it needs to be."

"I guess that's where we'll start, then." I move over to the nearest bookshelf and Milo follows.

"After you," he says.

"Thanks."

We walk the aisles together, each working on a different bookshelf as we go. "So, it must be nice getting back to work, right?" Milo asks.

"It is," I say. "It's nice leaving the house for something other than doctor appointments and food."

"I can't even imagine."

"What did you go through physical therapy for?"

The question falls out of my mouth before I can catch it.

"Oh, it wasn't anything serious." I turn to see the scarlet color he so often flashes spreading across his face again.

"You're blushing."

"What? No, I–" he sighs, throwing up his hands and letting them fall back to his sides, clearly flustered. "It's silly."

"I won't laugh, come on." What on Earth could have him so embarrassed?

He hesitates for a long minute, his words rushed together when he finally says, "I tripped over myself when I was a kid and broke my ankle."

A loud snort escapes my lips as I struggle to hold in my laugh. I close my eyes and clap my hand over my mouth, trying to regain my composure. "You, uh... you trip–you tripped over *yourself*?" I ask, my voice shaking from the restrained giggles.

He hangs his head in defeat. "Hey, I was twelve and I've always been a little clumsy, so..."

I allow one of the laughs to escape. "No, it's cu–it's funny," I catch myself. "But not like 'haha' funny. Like just–"

"Silly? Yeah, I know." He laughs with me and adds, "Yeah, okay, it's funny, too."

A couple walks in and Milo goes over to see if they need help with anything. He walks them over to the section holding biographies and pulls a book from the top. I keep working on the shelves in front of me as he walks them to the register.

A broken ankle by tripping over himself. Of all the things I had thought up to be the reason why he'd had physical therapy, that was not one of them. But, honestly, it fits him better than anything else I could've thought of.

"Yeah, you guys have a great day!" Milo calls to the couple as they leave the store. He walks back over to me and looks around like he's trying to remember where he left off. It doesn't take him long to figure it out.

"That was fast," I say.

"Hmm? Oh. Yeah, they just wanted that new biography about the local artists."

"I take it we had the one they wanted?"

"Of course. Everyone's favorite book store, right?" He stretches his arms out, mimicking Rob as he quotes him.

"That's pretty good," I say, giggling at his impression.

It's always nice when we have exactly what a customer is looking for. Being able to place that book in their hands and see their eyes light up has always been my favorite part of the job. It sucks when we can't make it happen for whatever reason.

"So what were we talking about again?" he asks.

"How you tripped over yourself and broke your ankle."

Milo frowns. "Oh, yeah. Well, what's the silliest thing you've ever done?"

I stop adjusting the books on the shelf and search my mind. What is the silliest thing I've ever done? "I don't know."

"There's got to be something."

"Uhh..." My mind is blank. I close my eyes, searching all the old archives in my head. "Oh! When I was six, I asked my mom what the llamas on Mr. Hannet's farm were. She told me they were horses that got their heads stuck in the fence. And I believed her."

Milo wastes only a second before roaring with laughter. "You believed her?"

"There's more," I say.

"More?"

I nod. "I got on the bus the next day and told all the other kids, too."

Tears are streaming down Milo's face. He's bent over, one hand clutching his knee and the other his stomach.

"It's not that funny, Milo," I say, laughing with him.

He straightens back up and wipes his tears. "Oh, no, it really is. I'm pretty sure that's the most adorable thing I've ever heard."

"It wasn't adorable. I didn't find out the truth for years!"

"Years?"

"Yes! I was in junior high when I learned the truth." We both laugh even harder, having to take a moment to let the giggles out before getting back to work.

"You didn't really believe that, did you?" he asks once the laughter calms down.

"I was six, Milo, what do you expect?"

"You were very gullible."

"I was six."

"Six to twelve, apparently." I glare and he adds, "I know I wasn't that gullible when I was six."

"No, you were just a hazard to yourself." I laugh as he hangs his head again.

A flurry of people enter the shop and we both set to helping them. The rush lasts about an hour, with Milo walking the sales floor and me taking care of things at the register.

"Do you need to take a break?" Milo asks after the

last customer leaves. He says it in a way that doesn't come off like he thinks I'm fragile or incapable of caring for myself.

"I could sit for a moment," I admit, relaxing onto the stool we keep behind the register.

"Do you need anything? A soda? A water? A sandwich?" He takes a backward step toward the rear of the store.

I grin and tell him, "If you want to grab me a water from the back, I'd appreciate it."

He turns around and takes off to the back of the store faster than necessary, tripping over his feet as he goes. He catches himself before he falls and continues on like nothing happened. I can't see his face, but I'm betting he's already blushing.

He's back in a minute and I can see that I was right—traces of red still remain. "Here you go," he says, holding out the bottle.

"Did you, uh—"

"Don't say it."

Shaking my head with a smile, I open the bottle he handed me and take a long drink of water. Milo wanders back to the shelves we left off at, managing both sides while I take my break.

I rub the side of my leg, feeling the ache of exhaustion

in the muscles and a mild pang of anger at experiencing this so young. I've only been on my feet for a few hours. I shouldn't be having issues like this at only eighteen.

"So what do you plan to do now that you're done with high school?" Milo asks. He's made it over to the bookshelves near me and is straightening them while he talks.

I think about his question and realize that I don't know anymore. Before the accident, it was easy. Lilah and I were going to go to Oakvale. She was going for accounting, me for education. I had everything planned out for us. But now? Without Lilah... I don't know when I could bring myself to go.

Or if I even still want to.

Besides, Mom is here. And when she wakes up, I want to be here, too.

"You don't have to answer," Milo says, his voice soft. I'm not sure how long I was lost in thought.

"I wanted to be a teacher." I do him a favor and don't say any of the other things floating through my mind.

He doesn't miss my phrasing, though. "Wanted? As in, you don't anymore?"

"I don't know what I want anymore."

He changes the subject, seeming to pick up on my

mood much like Dylan does. "What's your middle name?"

A grin tries to come through. "Are we playing 'Twenty Questions' now?"

"Sure, I love that game," he says, clearly meaning it.

I sigh, shaking my head, but thankful for the change of direction. "Jane."

"Jane?" he asks. "You don't look like a Jane."

I nod. "My mom saw it in a magazine. She was reading some article about a house fire that had happened in town, and the writer was named Jane." Milo stops what he's doing and turns to stare at me. "What?"

"So... you got your middle name from a house fire?"

"No, that's not what I said. The woman who wrote the article–"

"Yeah, but if the house fire hadn't happened, your mom might not have seen that writer's name." He grins and adds, "You were named after a house fire."

I roll my eyes, dropping my head into my hands. "I was not named after a house fire." I look back up at him, knowing it's my face that's red this time.

He laughs, holding both hands up in front of him. "Alright, alright. Whatever you say, House Fire."

"Oh, please don't call me 'House Fire'." I pause,

groaning at the idea. Then ask, "What's your middle name? No, actually, how did your parents come up with 'Milo'?"

"Well, it wasn't a house fire," he mumbles. "But, it isn't much better, either."

I smile, leaning over the counter and resting my chin on my hands. "Go on."

He gives a long exhale and says, "My parents named me after the dog they had when they first got together."

I bite my lip, the laughter right behind it. "You were named after a dog?"

"I should have thought about that before I said you were named after a house fire, huh?"

"Yeah, I'd say so. And now I have to know your middle name."

"It's Oliver."

"Isn't that the name of the dog from that cartoon?" I can't remember the movie, but Milo seems to know what I'm talking about.

"No, that was the cat's name."

"Your parents just wanted to name you after animals, didn't they?" I giggle.

"Actually, Oliver is my dad's name, House Fire," Milo says, pretending to be offended.

I roll my eyes again. "You've got to come up with a better nickname."

"How about Little Elle?"

The emotion hits me faster and harder than I expect, but I keep my composure. "No, that's what my mom calls me."

"Lowercase it is, then," he says.

A slow grin claims my lips, pulling me away from my feelings. "Lowercase?"

"Yeah, like a little letter 'L'." He pinches his fingers together in front of one squinted eye.

"I think I'm okay with that one."

"What about me? Are you going to start calling me 'dog' or 'trip' or something?"

"I'll probably just stick with 'Milo' if that's okay with you."

I expect him to protest, but he gives a shy grin instead. "Yeah, I think I'm okay with that, too."

I turn away from him, looking at the clock on the wall. Three hours isn't bad for a first day back. I pull out my phone and send Dylan a text. She almost instantly replies, saying she'll be here soon.

"I think I'm done for the day."

Milo frowns for only a moment, barely enough to glimpse it. "Do you need me to call your Dylan–your Aunt?" His fumble is cute.

"No, I just texted her. But thank you."

"Yeah, no problem." Milo runs one of his hands through that messy hair of his. "It was really great getting to work with you today, Ellessy."

My name sounds nice on his lips. "Yeah, you, too."

Milo follows me to the back, holding the door open so I can clock out. I glance at his timecard as I'm putting mine back. His last name is Fellows.

Milo Fellows. It suits him.

Dylan is waiting out front when we return. She must have been hanging out nearby, just waiting for me to let her know when I was ready. Knowing Dylan, that's probably exactly what she was doing.

Milo rushes over to hold the door open for me as I leave. "See you later, *Lowercase*."

I smile. "See you later, Milo."

Twelve

Mom still hasn't had any improvement. Her nurses have tried to explain how things are going with her in words that are over my head, but I'm catching enough to understand that they aren't sure when she'll wake up. Or if she will. But that's not something I want to think about.

"I went back to work yesterday," I say, tracing circles around the knuckles on Mom's hand. "I wasn't sure how long I'd be there, but I stayed three hours and even helped during a rush." Take some of my determination, Mom, please.

"Dylan stayed close by so she could be ready to pick me up as soon as I texted her I was ready." I stroke away a piece of hair that's matted to her face. I wish there was a way to wash her hair better. "Mom, I know you think she's just like him, but she's not."

I look over my shoulder at Dylan. She's sitting on the bench in the hall outside Mom's room, working the crossword in today's paper. "She's actually really great, Mom. She's been there for me this whole time, and... I don't know that I could've gotten this far if she hadn't been here." I turn back to mom and lean in closer. "I think Dylan should stay with us when you wake up. I fought so hard to get well enough so you wouldn't have to see her, but now I don't want her to leave, Mom."

My lower lip starts to tremble, but I fight it back. If she's one of those patients that remembers what was said to her, I don't want all of her memories to include me crying.

I wipe away the few tears that made it out and clear the emotion out of my throat. "So, yeah, I went back to work yesterday. Rob and Martha kept my job for me, and they, uh, they let me come back whenever I was ready, so..." I turn over her hand and start tracing my finger along the lines in her palm. She's always hated that. Maybe she'll wake up and tell me to stop. "They had me working with the new hire."

I turn her hand back over and squeeze it. "He's a nice guy. Dylan swears he has a crush on me, but… you're here and Lilah's gone, so…" I take a deep breath, shaking my head before blurting, "He's named after a dog." A small giggle escapes, followed by immediate guilt.

It feels strange laughing next to mom when she's like this. I know she'll be annoyed when I admit that to her years from now. She always prefers smiles to sadness. But how can I sit here and smile when she can't even breathe on her own? When Lilah can't breathe at all?

I clear my throat again. "He is really nice, though. I liked working with him."

Someone speaking in the hallway draws my attention. Mom's nurse is talking to Dylan. Judging by their body language, it's the same conversation we get every time we come visit–she's stable but no real improvement, so we don't know when or if she might wake up. I don't need to hear the words to know what's being said.

I turn back to look at Mom. "Nothing new today, I guess." I lay my cheek on her hand and close my eyes. I breathe in, deep, trying to smell lazy Saturday mornings snuggled up on the couch. All I get is medical supplies and cheap detergent.

Mom's favorite song pops into my head and I start humming it. Her chest rises and falls in a near perfect beat with the tune.

It shouldn't be like this.

I turn her palm to my cheek and squeeze my eyes shut tight, willing her to wake up and hold my face for real.

I stay like this for a while. My left leg starts to tingle from the position I'm sitting in. I wonder if Mom's hand is asleep from my cheek resting on it for so long? Would she know if it was? Would it bother her?

Would it make her wake up if I laid on it long enough?

I stand up and lean over her bed to kiss her forehead. "I love you, Mom," I say, my voice croaking out in a whisper. I clear my throat and try again. "I love you, Mom." I kiss her forehead one more time, lingering a second longer than last time. "I'll see you soon."

Dylan stands as she sees me walking toward the hallway. "You ready to go, kiddo?" she asks.

I watch Mom's chest rise and fall one more time before I nod and turn to leave.

I check my phone when we get out to the SUV. There's a text from Abbie and one from Milo. "Abbie wants to know if she can come by later."

"Yeah, tell her to come hungry and I'll make dinner," Dylan says. I grin and send the reply.

I open Milo's text.

> Hey! How are you? :)

I send a quick reply.

> I'm okay... You?

"Who you talkin' to?" Dylan tries to sneak a quick peek at my phone.

"You already know who I'm talking to, I'm sure." I point to the road and add, "Eyes out there."

Another reply from Milo comes through.

> I'm good! Was thinking about rereading that poetry book I showed you. Have you read it yet?

I laugh internally, shaking my head. He must really want someone to talk to about this book or something.

> No, not yet. I might tonight if I have time. Abbie is coming over.

"What are we having for dinner?" I ask.

> That sounds fun! Tell Abbie hi for me. And let me know if you end up reading it. I don't know how fast you read, but it never takes me too long to get through it.

"Oh I'll probably make pork chops and mashed taters," Dylan says. "Does that sound good to you?"

> How many times have you read it?

"Yeah, that sounds good."

> … A few…

"Do you know if Abbie would like that?"

> Lol well I'll let you know if I read it.

I think about it and realize that I'm not sure what she normally likes to eat. "I don't know, I'll text her." I send a quick text to Abbie and she replies shortly after. "She said that's fine."

Milo texts me again.

> I hope you do! Anyway, have fun tonight. :)

Dylan gets into the turning lane. "Guess we better stop off at the grocery store and get a few things, then."

> Thanks. :)

I hesitate before sending it, not sure how I feel about the smiley face. It feels dumb to question something like that, but it feels weird to type it out after just having spent a few hours talking to my comatose mother.

I hit send anyway.

We make a quick run through the grocery store, grabbing food for tonight and a few extra things like soda and some cookies from the bakery. Dylan winks at me. "Might as well, right?"

Dylan starts cooking as soon as we get home. "Do you want any help?" I ask her.

"No, ma'am," she says. "This is my area right now, so you just scoot on out of here." She waves me out of the room as she starts making more of a mess than anything. The kitchen always looks like chaos when she sets her mind to making dinner, but something good always comes out of it.

I head down the hall and into my room, flopping down on my bed and sinking into the pillow. It'll probably be another hour before Abbie gets here and Dylan has dinner ready.

I grab Milo's poetry book from the stack next to my bed. With nothing else to do while I'm waiting, I might as well get some reading in.

I devour the book in thirty minutes. It's been a while since I've read anything, let alone something that had me turning pages like that. He wasn't wrong when he said it was really good.

I pull out my phone and go to the message thread with Milo's name.

> I read it.

As fast as he responds, you'd think he somehow knew I'd been reading it and was just waiting for my text.

> AND?!

I grin.

> I loved it.

He replies in seconds. If his texts could show

emotion, I'd swear he's jumping up and down right now.

> Yay! I knew you would. Which poem was your favorite?

I pick it back up and flip through the pages, trying to decide which one spoke to me the most.

> The one about the lion.

Another text comes as I read through the poem again.

> I really like that one, too. :)

> Which one was yours?

I fan through the pages, trying to make a guess before he replies. I'm not fast enough.

> I like them all. You can't make me pick just one!

I laugh and roll my eyes.

> Why did you ask me which one was mine then? Lol

I don't know why I'm surprised.

> I was curious if you could pick a favorite lol

I hear a knock at the front door followed by Abbie's voice as Dylan opens it.

> Abbie's here. I'll talk to you later.

I get up and head for the kitchen.

> Okay :)

"Hey, Ellie," Abbie says, pulling me in for a hug, careful not to spill the drink in her hand. "Mmm, something smells good in here, right?" She pulls away and takes a deep breath, exaggerating the motion.

I smile. "It does."

Abbie holds up the drink she brought. It's from the place where we get the sweet teas I like. "Dylan said you've been craving these lately?" She holds it out to me.

"Yeah, she's been suckin' those down like they're goin' out of style," Dylan says.

I take the drink from Abbie. "Thank you."

"We shoulda got some tea to make here at home, Elle," Dylan says, opening one of the cabinets on the wall. She moves a few things aside before closing it. "Yeah, I don't see any tea bags in here. Remind me next time we go and I'll pick some up."

"I don't think I'm the one likely to remember out of the two of us."

Dylan grabs the notepad we normally write the grocery list on. "On the list it goes." She writes it down and goes back to cooking.

"Do you want me to go ahead and set the plates out, Dylan?" Abbie asks.

"Nonsense. You're the guest." Dylan waves her away. "Both of y'all just sit down and I'll get things finished up here."

I move over to the cabinet where we keep the plates and pull three out. Dylan starts to say something but I cut her off. "I'm not a guest, so don't say anything." She scowls, but keeps her comments to herself as I pile silverware on top of the stack.

"Let me help you, Ellie." Abbie grabs the silverware and places them next to the plates as I set them down.

"You're about as stubborn as she is," Dylan says, grumbling to herself more than anyone.

"So are you," Abbie says, laughing.

"It comes with age," Dylan says. "Now, go on and sit. Dinner's almost cooked." Abbie and I do as we're told this time, sitting at the table as Dylan sees to finishing the food.

"So, how was your day, Ellie?" Abbie asks, turning to me.

"We went to go see Mom today."

"Oh, that's good. I know how much that must mean to you, to have time to visit with her." She doesn't ask how Mom is doing, which is honestly nice. I don't like having to explain that there isn't anything new to say and I don't have any of the answers I desperately want.

"Yeah."

"You texted right as we were leaving, actually," Dylan says. She scoops the pork chops out of the skillet and onto the plate lined with paper towels next to her. She shuts the burner off and brings the plate to the table.

"Boy, those look good." Abbie scoots her chair closer to the table.

"Oh, they will be," Dylan says. She tosses a few pot holders on the table and sets the pot with mashed potatoes on top of one. "I hope you came hungry, 'cause Elle doesn't do leftovers."

"Sometimes I do."

Dylan gives me a look that says she's not buying it

as she sets two more pots on the other pot holders, one with gravy and the other with hominy.

She's right, though. I don't like leftovers. Something that has always annoyed Mom, too. Another thing they have in common.

"Well you can send them home with me," Abbie says. "I'm still living like a college student, so this is a feast for me."

Dylan pulls a baking sheet full of biscuits out of the oven and shuts it off. She grabs a mixing bowl out of the cabinet, casually tossing all the biscuits in after. She brings it over to the table and finally joins us.

"You didn't have to go all out," Abbie says, eyes wide over the meal.

Dylan snorts. "I didn't."

"We got cookies, too." I point to the package on the counter.

"I feel like I should have brought something."

"Nonsense." Dylan passes her one of the pots. "Now fill your plate. There's plenty to go around."

We pass around the food, filling our plates and wasting no time digging in.

"So, when are you thinking you'll come back for another shift, Ellie?" Abbie asks. "Milo told me you did really good on your first day."

"I was hoping I could come back tomorrow or the

day after," I say. I wonder if she asked Milo about it or if he told her on his own.

"That's great. Just don't push yourself too much, okay? There's plenty of time to get back into the swing of things."

"I've been tryin' to tell her," Dylan says around a mouthful of mashed potatoes.

"I'm learning my limits." And I have to push them if I want things to get back to normal.

Dylan seems to know what I'm thinking. "Learn 'em and push 'em, but don't haul off and break 'em."

Abbie points at me with her fork. "Exactly."

"I'll be fine. I'm not there by myself, anyway."

"Milo seems very taken by you," Abbie says, grinning. "He stopped in for something during my shift today, and his face lit up when I mentioned you." That must be when he told her about my shift.

"She knows," Dylan says. "Those two been textin' and I told her she's blind if she can't see he's got a crush."

I feel the heat in my cheeks. "We're just friends."

"Aw, well I think he's a great young man for you to be friends with, Ellie."

Dylan and Abbie continue talking about Milo and work and other stuff I space out on. I smile and do my best to pitch in where I can, but they mostly drive the conversation between themselves during the rest of dinner.

I finish eating first and get up to put my plate and silverware in the sink. "I'm going to go read for a bit before I fall asleep." I gesture toward the hallway. "It was nice to see you, Abbie."

"Yes, it was so great getting to come over and chat with you, Ellie." She stands and holds out her arms for a hug. "I work tomorrow, so I can talk to Martha about getting you in for another shift, okay?"

"Thanks." I smile and turn to Dylan. "Thanks for dinner."

Her mouth is full, so she just nods and waves it away like she does with most compliments and thank yous.

I head back to my room and change into pajamas, ready to relax.

Or try to, anyway.

I crawl into bed and grab another book off the pile.

Thirteen

> Martha said you might be working with me today?

It's been a few days since dinner with Abbie. She kept her word and mentioned to Martha that I wanted to come in and work again soon. Today is the day.

> Yeah, I'll be there in about half an hour.

Milo is working with me again. I don't know if it's coincidence, or if Abbie said something to Martha about scheduling me on one of his shifts, but here we are.

> Awesome! I think it'll be another slow day. There's some kind of book signing at a shop in Wynette, so most of our regulars will be over there.

I wonder if he'll have everything done before I get there again.

"I'm ready to go when you are, Dylan," I call from the kitchen. She's upstairs in the guest bedroom. I guess at this point we might as well just call it her room. Especially if I can get Mom to give Dylan a chance when she finally wakes up and we can actually talk about it.

"Yeah, I'm comin' kiddo," Dylan says as she comes down the stairs. "Somebody used all the warm water again today, so it took me a mite longer to feel fresh." She arches a brow at me, but grins at my wide-eyed reaction.

"Sorry, Dylan. I guess I don't realize how long I spend in there." I know I spend a lot of my time in the shower just letting the water stream over me like it's washing away the things I don't want to think about, but I didn't think about just how long that might be.

"Well, let's go. I'm sure you wanna stop and get a tea before you head in today."

"Yes, please." I smile and head out the door.

We get to the bookshop–tea in hand–a short while later. I wave goodbye to Dylan and walk up to the front door, which Milo is holding open.

"Welcome to work today," he says.

"Thanks, Milo." I walk past him, heading to the back so I can clock in. Looking around, I can see that the store is in perfect condition. "No customers so far?"

"Just a few. Like I said, with that book signing in Wynette, most of our regulars are over there." He follows me to the back, waiting in the doorway again.

"You made use of the extra time, I see." I fill out the sheet and we head back to the front.

"I might have gotten here a little early to have everything done before you got in."

I whip around to look at him. "Seriously?"

Milo's face glows red, but he's quick to say, "Well, I didn't intend to get *everything* done. Just all the backroom stuff like last time... but..." he gestures around the shop. "The only two customers we've had came in for a specific book, so..." He shrugs.

"Well, I guess it'll be an easy day for me, then." I shake my head and laugh. "Do Rob and Martha know how fast you get things done around here?"

He smiles and nods. "Yeah, they keep telling me they're not gonna let me go when I finish college."

He's going to college. I wonder where. "College?"

"Yeah, I go to Kassemme. I was worried I'd have to beg Rob and Martha to let me stay when I start going somewhere else for my bachelor's, but I don't think it will be a problem." He laughs again and adds, "I've never liked the idea of moving too far away from my little sister, so I'm sure I'll pick somewhere close by."

Kassemme isn't by any means a big city, but it's definitely a large enough town to have a community college. Lilah and I both applied and got accepted, but it's not where we wanted to go. The plan was always Oakvale.

"You'll be graduating soon, won't you?" Milo is older than me, but I'm not sure how much.

"Yeah, I've got one more semester. I couldn't quite get it all done in two years." He frowns. "Are you planning to go? You just graduated, right?" I wonder for a second how he knows, but I imagine Abbie or Martha probably said something.

Or maybe he read one of the articles about my car accident.

"I did. And I was accepted to Oakvale." I move over to sit in one of the chairs by the front window nook.

"I thought about going there for my bachelor's."

Milo sits in the chair across from me, looking excited over this news.

"I don't think I'm going anymore."

"Did I scare you away?" He laughs, rubbing the back of his neck.

I smile, but I'm sure the sadness is plain behind it. "Lilah and I were supposed to go together." My voice breaks a little–barely enough to notice. "I don't think I can do it without her."

"Lilah was your best friend, right?" he asks, the energy from before gone.

I nod. If I try to say anything more, I'm afraid I'll cry. Something about using her name and talking about her in past tense makes it more real. And when it's more real, I can't ignore it anymore.

"You could always reapply later on down the road if you wanted." He gives me a warm smile and changes the subject. "So is poetry your favorite?"

I'm thankful for the change. "I don't know that it's my favorite, but I really like to read it."

"Same. My mom used to read it to me before bed, so I guess I was raised on it." He stands up. "I'll be right back."

He heads to the back of the shop, returning a few moments later with a bottle of water. "I would have grabbed you one, but you have a drink already," he says, sitting across from me again.

"Thanks anyway," I say. With there usually only being one person here during the week, I'm suddenly wondering why we've never thought to put a mini-fridge behind the register. I might have to talk to Dylan about her plans for the one she got from the silent auction. It's been in her room since we brought it home, but she's rarely in there. It might be more useful here. "We should put a mini-fridge behind the register."

Milo glances over there. "That's not a bad idea."

"I have those sometimes."

"Bad ideas?" He turns back to me, grinning.

I roll my eyes. "So what are you going to college for?"

"Occupational Therapy."

"What's that?"

He's clearly excited to explain. "It's kind of like what you did with physical therapy, but instead of focusing on the problem, it's more like helping the person do things even with the problem." He shakes his head and adds, "I'm really bad at explaining it."

"I think I get it." It's nice that he wants to help people like that. "Did your, uh, *incident* have anything to do with that career choice?" His face turns red at the vague mention of his tripping over himself as a kid. My smile gets a little wider as I realize just how often I make him blush.

"Maybe a little. Mostly I just want to help people and that seemed like a good way to go." He shrugs. "That's probably a silly way to pick your career."

"No, I think it's good. Not everyone needs a big backstory for their big decisions."

"What about you? What do you want to be when you grow up?" He chuckles at his wording.

"I always thought I'd be a teacher."

He squints at me like he's trying to picture it. "Yeah, I think I could see that."

"Really?"

"Yeah, why? Do most people not think so?"

"No, it's not that. Just... No one besides my mom has ever told me I'd be good at it. Not even Lilah."

"Really?" He seems more surprised this time.

"Yeah, she thought I should get a business degree, run my own store."

"I could see that, too." He squints at me again. "So what's the big backstory behind wanting to be a teacher?"

"Lucky for you, I do have a backstory," I say.

"Oooh." He leans forward, resting his chin in his hands.

"I never really had a lot of friends other than–other than Lilah..." My voice catches and I take a moment to clear my throat before rushing through the rest. "And my teachers were always really nice and made me feel special when the other kids told me I wasn't. And, uh... I want to be that person for someone else."

Milo is quiet for a long moment. "You're a really good person, you know that?"

I can feel the blush coming before it hits me. The more I try to cover it with my hands, the warmer my face grows. I give up and ask, "What's your next question?"

He grins. "What's your favorite color?"

I laugh–a good, loud laugh. The kind I haven't laughed in a while. "It's blue."

"Don't most teachers like yellow?"

I snort. "I'm not a teacher."

"But you will be someday."

"I might be."

"You will." He looks determined enough for both of us. "Mine's green, by the way. In case you were wondering."

"Oh, thanks for that information. It definitely changed my day." My playful sarcasm thankfully doesn't go over his head.

"You know what, I knew it would." He grins. "Alright, your turn. Ask a question."

A customer rushes in and looks around, clearly confused. They spot us and ask, "Is this where the book signing is?"

"No, you want to go to Sophia's Books 'n' Such in Wynette," Milo tells them. The customer thanks him and leaves. "It's been like this all morning before you got here."

"Who's doing the book signing?" I can't help but wonder why so many people knew about this but me.

"Some local who writes romance. Rob tried to get them in here, but apparently their tour was already booked or something." Milo shrugs. "That wasn't your question, right?"

"No. Uhh... What's your favorite food?"

"Like in general, or a specific item?" he asks, no indication that he's kidding.

"I didn't realize my question could have that many layers."

"I'll just answer it every way I can think of." He rubs his chin. "Okay. Breakfast, Chinese, soup, peanut butter sandwich." He counts them off on his fingers.

"None of those things make sense together."

"Right, well... Breakfast is my favorite meal of the day, but soup is my favorite type of food, even though peanut butter sandwiches are definitely my favorite thing to eat in the whole world."

I giggle. "Where does Chinese food fit in?"

"Well if you ask me if I want to go out for Chinese or sandwiches, I'm picking Chinese every time."

"I don't know how you managed to make all of that make sense, but I think you did."

"I like to make lists." He shrugs.

"So do I." My entire life is a list of plans. "It must be why you like the twenty questions game." I give him a big grin that he returns.

"So what's your favorite food, then?"

I think it over for a minute. "Breakfast for dinner, Italian, pasta, dinner rolls."

Milo claps and says, "I like these answers."

A rush hits the store before I can explain, likely all of the local customers returning from the book signing. The shop is filled with bubbly chatter and excitement as they wander around, showing off their goodies from the signing and seeing what books we had to offer that they hadn't found at the other store. Milo and I both move seamlessly through the crowd, helping them to find things and listening to their giddy tales of the day's event.

An hour goes by before we get through the crowd and the last person leaves. The store feels strange with the sudden emptiness after such a buzzing energy. I don't want to admit it, but I'm also tired from moving around as much and as long as I did. I sit back in the chair again, closing my eyes and letting out a long breath.

"I wasn't expecting that," Milo says, coming to sit down next to me.

I shake my head, "Me either." A yawn forces its way through.

"You can go home if you need to." He leans forward, looking both disappointed and concerned.

I really enjoyed talking with Milo today. Conversation flows fairly easy with him, and he seems to keep me distracted from the things I don't want to think about. It's nice, even if I know I'll feel guilty later.

I pull out my phone and send Dylan a text. "I need to clock out." I stand, Milo joining me.

"I can fill your time in."

Dylan was obviously hanging out nearby again. She pulls in before I can protest. "No, but thank you." I wave at Dylan and gesture to the back, hoping she'll understand what I'm doing.

"Let me get the door, at least." Milo rushes over and holds it open for me.

"Thanks," I say. My limp feels worse than normal, but I try to hurry to the back hall so I can clock out.

Milo waits for me in the doorway–as always–and then walks to the front door, keeping pace and paying no attention to the struggle in my left leg. He holds the door open for me again. "Do you mind if I text you later?"

I smile. "Yeah, that's fine."

His face lights up. "Okay. I'll talk to you later, then."

"Talk to you later, Milo." I say, quickly turning away from him. There's something awkward lingering between us and I'm ready to get away from it.

I walk to the SUV as fast as my tired leg will take me.

Fourteen

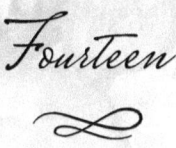

> Yeah, Martha said it's fine if you come in on Monday. That means you get to work with me again. :)

I shouldn't be feeling this. I have absolutely no business feeling anything like this right now. Lilah is gone and Mom still hasn't woken up, and I have no business feeling anything more than friendly feelings toward a guy I've only known for a couple of months.

It's not part of the plans.

> Great. Thank you for asking for me. :)

Guilt snakes its way down my spine and slithers down the length of my limbs. What is wrong with me?

"Did you still wanna go see your mama today, kiddo?" Dylan peeks her head into my bedroom.

"Yeah." I pull myself away from my thoughts, sitting up and swinging my legs off the side of my bed.

"Alright, go on and get ready, then. I need to get gas before we go and it's almost traffic time."

As much as I'm in my head and arguing with myself right now, I really don't want to be stuck in traffic. I slip on my shoes, grab my purse, and follow Dylan out the door.

We're lucky enough to get on the road and to the gas station before everyone leaving work gets on the road.

> Did I tell you I'm taking my sister to the zoo tomorrow?

>> I think so. That will be fun.

> Yeah I'm pretty excited. :)

>> You're always excited, Milo.

We hit a little bit of traffic on the way to the hospital, but nothing like we would have if we had left even just a few minutes later.

> Lol what are you up to? Any big plans for today?

> I'm visiting my mom. Text me later?

Sure!

Mom has a new nurse today. A younger guy I've never seen around before. He's overly nice, acting as if he has all of the answers, even when he doesn't have any at all.

I ask him if there have been any changes in Mom's condition.

"Your mom is doing really well, but we don't really have anything new to tell you." He says it like he's talking to a child.

I miss her other nurses.

He hangs out in the room a little longer than necessary. I step over by the wall and wait for him to do whatever it is he's needing to get done, trying my best to look anywhere but at him in case my eyes tip him off to my feelings.

I can feel the anxiety starting to ache in my chest.

He strings his checks along for every minute he can manage before finally saying, "All set," and leaving me alone with Mom. I glance at the nurse's board and catch his name. Micah. Even his handwriting looks like it's trying to prove something.

I scoot the chair around and pull it up next to the bed, thankful to finally be alone with her. "Hey,

Mom." Her pillow is crooked. All that time lingering and *Micah* didn't catch that. I adjust it before sitting down. "I hope he's treating you as well as your other nurses."

I shift awkwardly in my seat, realizing that I don't have much to talk about today. I want to spend time with her, to show her how much I've improved and encourage her to do the same. But there really isn't a whole lot to say.

My anxiety doesn't ease.

"I worked with Milo again," I say, the words coming out of my mouth slowly, like they're trying hard to stay tucked inside. "There was some kind of book signing for a romance author at that store over in Wynette–Sophia's Books 'n' Such. So it was pretty slow. We sat around talking for most of the shift." A smile claims my lips without permission. "He likes to play the twenty question game."

I chuckle to myself, forgetting for only a moment where I am. "I like working with him. He's easy to talk to, and funny, and really nice. I think you'll like him." Why did I say that?

I shift in my seat again, uncomfortable with myself and my emotions. This is not the time for my brain to be thinking about a guy.

It's not in the plans.

I let out a long breath, shaking the thoughts from my head.

I stand up and lean in close to Mom's ear, my voice barely a whisper. "When are you going to wake up, Mom?" My lower lip starts to tremble. I bite it, not willing to risk her hearing that emotion.

There's a harsh tap on the door that makes me jump. I turn around just as Mom's nurse, Micah, walks back in with one of her regular nurses following him. "Sorry to cut things short, but it's time to get your mother cleaned up." He smiles a sickly sweet smile and stands at the foot of Mom's bed, obviously waiting for me to leave.

I don't know why this needed to be done now, but I don't feel like asking. Micah isn't someone I want to talk to.

I turn back to Mom and kiss her on the forehead. I whisper, "I love you, Mom. We'll finish this talk soon."

Her regular nurse gives me an apologetic smile as I leave. Maybe no one here likes Micah. I'm sure he's probably a good nurse. Maybe he's just new and confident and wanting to make an impression. You'd think it would do him better to leave a good impression on the patients and their families, but what do I know?

I walk out to the hallway. Dylan is already standing, leaned against the wall with her arms crossed and one brow arched.

"I got kicked out."

"I heard." She shakes her head, opening her mouth as if to say something else, but shuts it, letting out a long breath instead.

She walks into the room and makes a point to look at the nurse's board, turning to me and saying, "We'll just come back another day."

Micah stares at her as she joins me in the hallway. We leave without another word.

"Thank you, Dylan."

"Don't worry about it, kiddo. Let's get outta here."

I hope that's one of the moments Mom remembers.

Dylan stops for food on the way home, making sure to go to the place with my sweet tea. She orders an extra, which turns out to be a good thing because I finish the first one before we even make it home.

I head back to my room, taking my food with me. Dylan doesn't say anything, of course. She sits at the table with her food and opens her crossword book to finish the one she'd started at the hospital. She never fails to sense my mood.

I eat my food and toss the trash into the trashcan

next to my bed, not even checking to make sure everything made it in. I don't care right now. I drop back on my pillow and close my eyes to the world, begging my mind to rest and not venture into those dark corners I'm desperate to avoid.

My phone vibrates and I seize the distraction. It's a text from Milo.

> Hey Lowercase. :)

That silly nickname.

> Hey Milo.

> Do you have any plans tomorrow?

Is he seeing if I want to work with him or something? I thought he already had plans tomorrow.

> No. Aren't you taking your sister to the zoo?

> She got a lead part in the musical her school is doing and they're having their first practice tomorrow.

There are two high schools here, one public and one Vo-Tech school where students can go to take special classes focused on a specific subject.

> Oh that's good that she got a lead part at least. Does she go to Kassemme High?

> Yeah she's a Freshman.

That's the school I graduated from, but Milo is only a few years older than me and I don't remember seeing him.

> Is that where you went?

> No, I went to Vo-Tech as soon as they would let me lol

That makes sense. I wonder if we would have been friends if we'd gone to the same school?

> What did you go to Vo-Tech for?

> I studied medical services. I thought it would help when I started applying for college lol

> Did it?

> I think so lol

He sends me another text.

> So would you want to go to the zoo with me tomorrow?

I stare at my phone's screen, rereading the message. Did he just ask me out?

Another message comes through before I can wrap my mind around the last one.

> Not a date! I just realized how that came off lol

I breathe a sigh of relief that doesn't really relieve anything. Three more messages pop up.

> I just don't want this extra pass to go to waste.
>
> Not that I wouldn't want to hang out with you otherwise!
>
> I'll stop now.

The tension in my shoulders eases as I picture the blush I know he has right now.

> I'll talk to Dylan.

> Okay! :)

Do I want to go to the zoo with Milo?

I get up and head into the kitchen. Dylan is doing the dishes. She looks up at me and asks, "You okay, kiddo?"

"Milo asked if I wanted to go to the zoo with him tomorrow."

Dylan grins. "I wondered when that boy would ask you out."

"It's not a date."

"Are you sure?"

I roll my eyes. "Yes, he told me it isn't. He was going to take his sister, but she can't go anymore."

"So when are you going?"

"He wants to go tomorrow."

"I heard that much. What time?"

"I don't know. He didn't say."

Dylan stops doing dishes and looks up at me again. "Do you want to go with him?"

I frown. "I don't know."

I wish I had Lilah here to talk to about this. I can hear her telling me to just go, can practically see her snatching my phone from my hand and texting him a "yes" for me.

I need my best friend.

I haven't actually been to see Lilah since–since her funeral. The guilt doesn't hesitate to form a knot in my stomach. I've been so caught up with getting better before Mom wakes up, that I haven't even thought about visiting Lilah. I got to survive when she didn't, and going to her grave hasn't crossed my mind even once.

The knot twists a little harder.

"I want to go see Lilah."

Dylan shuts the faucet off without a word and dries her hands. She grabs her things and holds the door open for me. "Let's do it."

The cemetery is prettier than I remember. Everything is green and well kept, not the dark blue that shades my memories. There are stone benches, and flowers adorn most of the headstones. For being a place of death, it sure looks pleasant here–almost happy.

"Do you remember where she's at?" Dylan looks around, squinting at the names on the stones.

"By the water, I think." The cemetery isn't huge by any means, but it's large enough to take all day to find a grave if you don't already know where it's at. There's one large pond over on the right side of the cemetery, with about twenty or thirty graves near it. I point to the tree nearest to the pond. "Over there."

We walk silently toward the water. I glance at the other headstones on the way. Most of them are older, probably having died of age related reasons. A few having only lived a few more years than Lilah. I wonder what happened to them. Did they die in car accidents?

Illness? From making silly little decisions they didn't realize would lead them right to the grave?

"What's her last name, Elle?" Dylan gets to the first sections of graves before I do.

"Day." I walk past the first row, straight to the headstones closest to the water. I can already see the one I know is hers.

There's a small headstone near the tree that looks a little newer than the rest. The ground in front of it doesn't quite have as much grass as the ones nearby. Emotion hits me when I see her name. *Lilah Shayne Day*. It hits even harder seeing the year she was born followed by this year underneath her name.

"Oh, Lilah..." My voice comes out on a breath as I crumble to my knees in front of her headstone. My fingers shake as I trace them along the letters of her name, willing them to change and none of this to be real. Wasn't it just a couple months ago that we were ready to head off to college? We're still babies. Babies aren't supposed to be broken and buried.

"I'm sorry." It blurts out of my mouth and continues on a sob, "I'm so sorry." My chest aches and my eyes are a blur of tears. I lie down on the ground above her, my ear pressed to the cold bits of grass trying to thrive on the recently disturbed dirt. I close my eyes and plead with my heart to stop beating so hard when Lilah's heart is lying useless just below us. How can my heart carry on like it's okay that I'm alive when she isn't?

I lay there like that for a while, six feet above her body and wishing I could just dig my way down and trade her places. But then what kind of selfish monster am I? Why would I wish for her to be the one up here, guilty and in pain? How is it right to wish our positions were reversed when I know she'd be right here crying over my body wishing the same? My gut feels twisted over the conflicting emotions. I don't know how to wrestle with wanting to give my life for hers while also never wanting her to feel the guilt and pain I feel being alive without her right now.

It isn't fair that she died and I didn't. I don't understand why it had to work out like this. I don't know how to get things right in my heart without tearing apart my mind.

The wind starts to blow, raising goosebumps on my arms. I open my eyes to see the sun saying its goodbyes to the day. "Dylan?"

"I'm here, kiddo." Her voice comes from the direction of the tree. I sit up and see her sitting on one of the stone benches overlooking the pond. She stands and puts her phone in her pocket.

"How long have we been here?"

Dylan reaches me and holds out a hand to help me get up. "A while." She dusts some dirt off my shoulder and shrugs. "It don't matter none to me. We can stay as long as you want."

I turn to look back at Lilah's name etched into her headstone. "We should've brought flowers."

"We will next time."

"But the fake kind. They don't die."

"What's her favorite?"

"Sunflowers," I say. "She likes sunflowers."

Fifteen

> Did you get a chance to talk to Dylan?

I never messaged Milo back yesterday.

"Milo still wants me to go to the zoo with him today."

Dylan glances up at me over her reading glasses, but keeps thumbing through the paperwork she has spread over the kitchen table. "And have you decided yet if you want to go?"

"I don't know."

"You don't have to go if you don't want to, kiddo." She takes her reading glasses off and sets them on the table, fully turning her attention to me. "But I think it would be good for you to get out of the house and have some fun with friends." She doesn't tease me about it being Milo.

"What if I get tired?" I'm stalling and we both know it.

"I'm sure I can find something to do nearby in case you need me."

"What if he thinks it's a date?" I grasp at straws I know aren't there.

She arches a brow. "Didn't he tell you it isn't a date?"

"Yeah."

"Then what are you worried about?"

I chew on my lip, trying to sort through my feelings. Why am I so hesitant? It's not a date. He's just a friend. And I enjoy hanging out with him at work.

So why shouldn't I go?

> I'll meet you there. Dylan is going to drop me off.

> Awesome! When do you want to meet? :)

> Are you free now?

> Yeah! Ready when you are. :)

I stand. "Okay."

"Okay let's go?"

"Yeah, let's go." I try to ignore the anxiety and text Milo instead.

> I'm on my way now.

Dylan stands and grabs her things. "Make sure you put on your walkin' shoes."

> I'll meet you there! I'm excited to hang out with you today :)

I pull on my tennis shoes and grab my purse.

> Me too.

The zoo is across town, but traffic is light, so we get there in about fifteen minutes. Milo is already waiting outside the front entrance when we pull up. I wonder how close he lives?

"Just message me when you need me, kiddo." Dylan gives me a warm smile as I get out of the SUV.

"I will." I wave at her as she drives off. Milo is lowering his hand when I turn around. I guess he had been waving, too. I'm not surprised.

He pulls two zoo passes out of his pocket and holds them in front of me. "Are you ready for the most fun you've ever had at a zoo?" He gives me a big, goofy grin.

I can't help but smile, hardly feeling the nervous energy anymore. "I haven't been here since I was a kid."

"A younger kid?" he asks, arching a brow.

"You're not that much older than me."

"I know." He puffs up his chest. "I'm just a more mature kid than you."

"Oh, whatever." I gently push him and he does his best to pretend I almost knocked him over.

We both laugh and head up to the entrance. Milo hands the passes to the woman at the booth. She hands him two bracelets and we head inside.

"Here, let me see your wrist." I hold out my arm and Milo fixes the paper bracelet around it. He holds up the other and asks, "Can you help me with mine?"

"Sure." My hands fumble, but I get the bracelet fixed around his wrist.

"So what do you want to see first?"

"Don't we need a map?" I turn, looking around for one.

"Nah, it's an adventure. You don't need maps on adventures."

My brow arches. "Isn't there a joke somewhere about men not liking maps?"

"There is, and your attempt at it has been noted." He grins again. "Let's start on this side and just work our way around." He heads to the right, toward the birds.

"So you've been here before?"

"Oh yeah," he says. "My parents used to bring me here all the time when I was younger."

Maybe there was a time when we were both here and never knew it? "Which animal is your favorite to see?"

"Oh the snakes for sure."

"The snakes?" I shiver. Snakes are far from my favorite. I've always disliked them. Not as much as spiders, but pretty close. "Why snakes?"

"Because I'm terrified of them."

I laugh, shaking my head. "That's a silly reason to call them your favorite."

"Well, which one is yours?"

I think about it for a second. "The otters."

He nods. "Adorable. And why are they your favorite?"

"Because they're adorable, like you said."

"Well, there you go," Milo gives me a triumphant smile. "Your reason is boring."

I scoff. "Boring?"

"Yeah, you just like them because they're cute."

"And why does that make yours better?" I press my lips together, trying to hide my amusement.

"Mine has danger."

I snort. "Danger?"

He nods, puffing out his chest. "Just a single layer of glass between me and my biggest fear."

"I prefer cute to danger."

"I'll give you credit," he says. "They are cute."

One corner of my mouth curls up. "Mmhmm."

"Did you want to eat while we're here? I'll pay." I start to respond and he rushes to add, "Still not a date or anything. This isn't a date. But I was planning to pay for my sister's lunch anyway, so..."

"I'm always hungry." I smile and add, "You don't have to pay for mine, though."

"Only if you're sure."

"I'm sure, Milo." I'm starting to like the way his name sounds when I say it.

"Alright, Lowercase."

My smile stretches wider.

The zoo isn't very large, but you could easily lose most of your day here and not realize it. We make our way to the food concessions, taking our time and stopping to see all the animals along the way. Milo seems especially amused by the giraffes. "Imagine if we could ride them like horses!" We talk easily, like always.

Conversation with Milo comes as simple as if I were speaking with Lilah.

The food court is a little crowded, but we manage to find a table with two free seats. The people here before us left their trash, so Milo grabs it and takes it to the nearby trash can, mumbling about some people being lazy and rude as he goes.

"I'll go get the food while you watch our table, if that's okay with you?"

"Yeah, that's fine." I start to sit down but remember I need to pay for my food. "Oh, wait. I didn't bring cash."

He pauses. "Would you be comfortable with me paying for lunch if I promise to let you buy cotton candy later?"

I think about it, a slow smile finding its way to my face. "I suppose that would be okay."

"Do you know what you want to eat?"

"Surprise me. I'm not that picky." Why did I say that? I am definitely picky.

Milo gets a mischievous grin. "Follow up question. How hungry are you?"

"Average to normal?"

"Like, normal for a bear or normal for a cat?" He uses his hands to show the size differences.

"Somewhere in between."

"Okay, got it."

I shake my head as he heads off to the concession stand closest to us.

My hands fidget of their own accord, fighting with the guilt I don't want to feel right now. I'm having a good time. Things with Milo have always been comfortable and easy at work, but they seem to be the same outside of that, too. And it's nice.

I know Lilah would be so thrilled I'm out with a guy right now. But it's so hard to shake the feeling that it isn't fair. She should be here with us–insisting on being the third wheel, making insinuations, and asking blunt questions that embarrass me.

Milo comes back over with a full tray of food. He sits across from me, setting the tray down on the table. "Okay, so I got us hot dogs with nachos. They didn't have sweet tea, so I got water instead. Did I do okay?"

My thoughts melt away. The look on his face is adorable. I don't know how else to describe it.

I put my hand over the side of my mouth that won't stop trying to grin. "Why nachos and not fries?"

His face falls. "You would have preferred fries?"

"No, nachos are good. Better than fries, I think." His face lights up again, relief obvious in his expression. "I just wouldn't have thought of it."

"I'm a nachos guy." Milo pulls his food closer.

"I don't think I've ever had them with a hot dog before."

"Well, then you have been missing out." He puts a nacho chip on his hot dog and dips the combo into the nacho cheese sauce. He takes a bite and makes a noise that I can only take to mean it was a very good decision.

I shrug and follow his lead, dipping my hot dog into the nacho cheese and popping a chip into my mouth afterward.

"Do you like it?" he asks, clearly anxious to hear my answer.

I chew slowly, pretending to really debate his question. "It isn't terrible," I tease.

He scoffs. "Of course it isn't."

"No, it's actually really good. It's different, but I like it."

He smiles and takes another big bite.

The conversation slows as we both enjoy our food.

"How is your mother doing? If... if you don't mind me asking. We don't have to talk about it, if you don't want to." His voice is soft, none of the spunk he had before shining through. It's clear that he cares in some way.

I move my now empty plate to the side. "She's... I don't really know, honestly. Nothing has changed.

She's just… there." I clear my throat and look up at him. It's the first time I've really talked to anyone about Mom since everything happened. It's weird but also kind of nice–like I'm letting out some built up pressure.

"No change means nothing bad, though, right?"

"I hope so." I can't bring myself to tell him that's one of those thoughts I've been avoiding. I push past it, adding, "I go and visit her and I talk with her and I've heard that people in comas can hear you and remember what you say, so I always tell her how much I need her, but…" My lip starts to tremble and I bite the emotions back.

"We don't have to talk about it." He starts to reach his hand forward, but stops. "But if she's anything like you, I know she's pushing hard to come home."

The smiles we had moments ago are gone, that weight sliding over my shoulders again. I'm not upset at the conversation. It's honestly been nice to talk to someone about Mom and not break down or feel awkward.

It's always easy to talk with Milo, even when we're talking about the things that hurt.

"I think my Mom will like you." I don't know why I say it. The words are out of my mouth faster than my brain can process them. They aren't wrong, though.

"You think she will?" He seems to like the thought.

"Yeah, I think so." I grab a napkin and wipe at my mouth, suddenly feeling like there has to be cheese or something on my face.

A slow grin spreads from ear to ear on Milo. "You think she'll like me."

I roll my eyes and toss the napkin at him. He laughs and stands, picking up the tray and placing all of our trash on top.

I stand and follow him.

"Where do you want to go next?" he asks as he empties the tray and sets it on top of the stack.

"I guess we need to go see your snakes." I shiver, cringing at the idea.

"What about your otters?"

"I think they're on the way back to the entrance after that."

The glee in Milo's eyes could be mistaken for a sparkler. "After you," he says, gesturing toward the path.

We see the big cats and the wolves on our way, Milo stopping to point out "bean toes" and try to get the wolves to howl with him.

The darker part of our earlier conversation is far from my mind by the time we reach the snake exhibit.

Milo pauses just before we get to the door. "Are you okay?" I ask.

He closes his eyes and takes a deep breath. He nods and says, "I always have to prepare myself for it." Looking at me with a smile stretched across his face, he adds, "I'm good. Let's do it."

Milo opens the door and holds it, gesturing for me to go in first. I shake my head, holding my hands up. "Uhn-uh. This is your fear to face. I'm just moral support." I grab the door and lightly push at his shoulder to go on inside. Milo takes another deep breath, shakes his head, straightens his back, and steps inside. I try to stifle my giggle as I follow behind him.

The building with the snakes isn't very big. The wall to the right has various glass panels placed to let us view the snakes behind them. The left side has a mural of a snake and a bench in front of it that I head straight for. I take a seat, the cold stone sending another shiver down my spine.

"You don't want to come look with me?" He gives me an exaggerated frown.

"I can see them just fine from here, Milo." He stands there, looking from me to the snakes and back. After a moment, he walks over and joins me on the bench. "What are you doing?"

"You said we can see them fine from here." He squints at the glass panels on the wall across from us.

"Go look at your snakes, Milo."

"I am." He smiles at me and continues squinting at them from here.

The snakes all look relaxed, lazing away the afternoon while people come in and stare at them. They don't look bothered. The people standing in front of their enclosures don't seem to make them uncomfortable—as if they have no care in the world at all. I can't help but feel a little pang of envy.

"We can leave if you want." I snap out of my thoughts. Milo is watching me.

Our eyes lock for a second longer than I mean to. I look away, saying the first thing that pops in my head. "So tell me the story behind your snake thing."

He doesn't immediately speak, but I don't look at him, either. "My family brought me here a lot when I was a kid. My sister is weird and loves snakes. Every time we'd get to this exhibit, I would stay outside with one of our parents, and my sister would always come out talking about this giant snake they had—that it was the coolest thing she'd ever seen."

My eyes scan for something cool rather than scary behind the panels in front of us. Milo continues, "My sister and I are pretty close, so I knew if she said it was that cool, I needed to see it."

"Even if you were afraid?"

"Especially if I'm afraid of it." I chance a glance at him and he's smiling. "But by the time I finally worked up the courage to go in there and see it,"

"It had...passed?" I can't bring myself to say the word, even if my mind immediately goes there.

"No, it had been transferred to another zoo or something."

"Oh." Even for a creature that scares me, I feel relief.

"Yeah, and I missed my chance. My fear made me miss my chance to see one of the coolest things ever."

"You sound like a motivational speaker."

We both laugh. "I just don't want fear to keep me from anything ever again."

His words hit me hard. He doesn't want his fear to keep him from anything ever again. Is that what I'm doing? Am I letting my fears keep me from things? Is my fear the real reason I'm resisting the feelings for Milo I'm trying so hard to ignore?

That familiar pressure fills my head too fast, spinning the world around me. I can see, but I can't focus on anything. Milo's hand grasps my shoulder. "Ellessy, are you okay?"

I try to tell him I'm fine, but the words don't come out the way I want them to. I'm not even sure what I say, but I know it can't be convincing.

The pressure in my head grows and I'm vaguely aware of Milo asking me to hand him my cell phone. "Come on, Ellessy, Dylan is on her way." He helps me up and we start walking.

I don't know how long it takes us to get to the entrance, or if we even have to wait for Dylan to get there. I can't breathe. I can't think. Everything is speeding past me and I can't grab on long enough to know what's real.

I don't even say bye. I don't hear what Milo says to Dylan. I don't even know how I get in the SUV.

I close my eyes, stumbling through my ABCs in a desperate attempt to slow my mind down. Over and over, forwards and backwards so that I'm forced to focus on anything other than that pressure that won't fade.

Dylan talks to me as she drives. I don't hear what she's saying, but her voice is enough. Things start to slow down. The world stops trying to leave me behind.

I can breathe again.

Sixteen

"I'll be over here when you're ready, kiddo."

"Okay," I say, sitting down on the ground in front of Lilah's headstone.

Dylan heads over to the bench she'd found last time we were here and settles in with one of her crossword books.

"Here." I pull the dead flowers out of the vase in front of me, tossing them to the side and replacing them with the sunflowers we got on the way here. "I got the fake ones so you don't have to worry about them dy–you won't have to worry about them."

My phone vibrates and I glance at it long enough to see Milo sent me a picture of a cat in a suit. I slide my phone back into my pocket and clear my throat, an awkward ache rising in my chest. "I guess we need to talk about that, don't we?"

I look out across the lake. The wind is blowing a little today, but it isn't cold at all. Typical for August.

I close my eyes and take a long breath. When I open them again, they fall right to her name on the headstone. Lilah Shayne Day.

I hate seeing that name there.

I feel my phone vibrate again and just ignore it.

"It isn't fair, Lilah." I pick at the grass around her headstone, my hands trying to keep busy for my mind. "We had plans. I had our whole future planned for us. And I know you said that some things just happen, and I know you wanted to fall in love right away, but a boy was not supposed to be in the picture."

I pause, hearing Lilah's voice in my mind, knowing what she'd say if she could reply.

I told you so, Ellessy.

"I know. And I know I'm being dumb."

I still love you.

"But it isn't fair to you."

Okay, now you're being dumb.

"How can I think about having feelings for someone when I told you we were waiting and now–"

And now what?

"And now you're gone and can't have it at all?"

Don't use me being dead to get out of falling in love.

My lip trembles as my mind supplies the words. If I didn't know better, I might think it's really her.

I stop picking at the grass. "I don't know how to be happy right now."

But you like him.

"I like Milo."

And he likes you.

"I think he does." A shiver hits me and I'm not sure if it's our conversation or the wind. Am I really admitting that Milo and I have obvious feelings for each other?

Am I really admitting it to Lilah? Right here at her grave?

I swallow the lump trying to form in my throat and I go back to pulling bits of grass.

"We went to the zoo a few days ago. And it was a great time... until my anxiety got the best of me and I couldn't think or breathe. And he was great, Lilah. He didn't freak out or run. He just called Dylan and helped me get to her. I ruined the day and he still texted me all night."

A slow smile grows as I think about the four texts I woke up to that evening.

> Dylan told me you were having a panic attack and would be fine, but I wanted to check on you anyway.
>
> Are you okay?
>
> You're probably sleeping.

And then one more that said:

> I hope you're okay.

When I finally woke up and replied, we talked for the rest of the night.

"He makes me smile." My grin widens for just a moment before completely disappearing. "Why am I even entertaining the thought now when I refused to while you were ali–when you were alive?"

Why would that matter?

"How is it fair to you if I change my mind now that you're gone?"

How is it fair to me that you're trying to live like you're the one who died?

I suck in a breath.

I know it's not really her speaking in my head, but the words hit me hard. She's right. Or, my mind's version of her is. I'm living like I died right along with her—holding myself back from things, feeling like I'm not allowed to be happy anymore.

And the real question I should be asking is, how is that fair to her?

I feel so much guilt for surviving, that I haven't stopped to think about the guilt I should be feeling for living like I didn't.

I take a deep breath, weighing our conversation in my mind. "Okay, Lilah." You're right. Of course, you're right, you always are. And I am hearing it loud and clear. I can't keep living like this.

"It's time to change the plan."

I stand up, grabbing the dead flowers as I do. "Thanks for still being there, Lilah." I make one more adjustment to the sunflowers in her vase and add, "I love you."

Dylan looks up before I make it halfway over to her. "You ready?" she asks.

I nod. "I'm ready."

"We can stay longer if you want."

"No, I'm ready." My tummy grumbles.

"Sounds like you're hungry, too. We can grab something to eat on the way home."

"Okay."

We don't talk as we walk back to Dylan's SUV.

There's so much on my mind, and I'm still trying to process everything.

I glance back toward Lilah's grave as I climb into the front seat. A breeze ruffles the leaves near the pond, sending a few spiraling out over the water.

Don't use me being dead to get out of falling in love.

I put on my seatbelt and pull out my phone.

"Where do you wanna eat, kiddo?" Dylan pulls away from the cemetery, but waits at the stop sign for me to offer a suggestion. She gives one when I don't. "Burgers and tea?"

I pull up the text conversation with Milo, not even glancing at Dylan as I say, "Yeah, that sounds fine."

"Something on your mind?"

"Mmhmm." We still haven't moved yet, so I look at Dylan. "Good things, I think."

She grins and takes a left.

I realize that I don't really know what to say. My thumbs hover above the letters, waiting for the right words to come. I decide to start simple.

> Hey.

As is usual for Milo, it doesn't take him very long to reply.

> Hey! How are you? :)

I pause again, feeling awkward.

> I'm good. I've been thinking about things and wanted to talk to you.

My heart feels like it's holding its breath in my chest.

> Is everything okay? Is this about the other day at the zoo? Are you sure you're okay after all of that?

A grin starts forming and I bite my lip. I can feel Dylan glancing at me every few minutes and don't want to feed the story I know she already has playing out in her head.

> Yes everything is fine Milo lol

> Okay good. You had me worried lol

> Don't worry.

> No guarantees, House Fire ;)

> I told you not to call me that, Boy Who Trips Over Himself.

> Aww I'm never going to live that down am I?

This time I can't hide the grin.

> Do you want to hang out?

> I'm at work right now and I have to help my parents with something tonight, but yeah! We could do something tomorrow if that's cool with you? :)

I take a second to try and figure out how to word my reply, anxiety tearing at every idea.

> Do you like me as more than friends?

My stomach drops as soon as I hit send. What did I do? What if we're all wrong and he doesn't even like me?

A full minute passes before Milo replies with one word.

> Yes.

I let out a long breath, relieved to cross the first hurdle unharmed.

Another wave of anxiety comes over me as I push on to the next message.

> That's how I want to hang out.

I almost don't hit send, but I push the button before I can talk myself out of it.

His reply takes just long enough to raise goosebumps across my arms.

> Are you asking me to hang out as more than friends?

I chew on my cheek as I type.

> I am.

> Are you sure that's what you want? I really wasn't trying to pressure you into anything you're not ready for, Ellessy. The zoo was not meant to be a date if it came off like one.

Texts like this are the reason girls like me–who don't plan for things like this–end up giving them a chance.

> I like you.

> I really like you too.

My heart thumps a little harder.

> Do you still want to hang out tomorrow?

> Yeah! I mean, only if you're really sure that's what you want.

I chew on my lip a little harder. How do I word this without sounding crazy?

> I don't want to rush into anything. But I like you and I can't pretend that it's only as friends. So…yeah. I want to try a real date this time.

It sounded smooth in my head, but rereading the text, I'm not so sure.

> A real date. :)

He sends another text right after that one.

> The zoo wasn't a date though.

> It kind of was. We just didn't know it yet.

I regret that message as soon as I send it, feeling like the biggest dork.

He sends two more texts.

> If you say so, Lowercase. :P

> So where do you want to hang out tomorrow? What time? Do you want me to pick you up? Sorry lol I'm really excited to see you again. :)

"Dylan?" I finally tear my eyes away from our conversation and turn to her. She's clearly doing all she can to pretend she hasn't been peeking at my phone this whole time.

"Hmm?"

"Do we have any plans tomorrow?"

"You weren't planning to go to work?"

"Not tomorrow, no."

"Then I'd say the whole day is free for you to do what you want with it, kiddo." She pulls into the drive through. "You got something you're wantin' to do?"

I dive back into texting as the girl asks for our order.

> How about the mall? We could walk around and eat at the food court?

> Definitely! What time? Is Dylan bringing you?

"Elle?"

"Yeah, can we go to the mall tomorrow?"

"Anything in particular you're wantin' there?"

I try to say it as casually as possible "I've asked Milo

out. To the mall." I nibble on the inside of my cheek again. "On a date."

"Ha!" Dylan slaps one hand against the steering wheel, startling the girl waiting to take her card. "I knew it, I just knew it."

I cringe, sinking my face into my hands. "Can I tell him I'll be there?"

"Hoo, you shoulda told him five minutes ago!"

If I've ever wondered if a person could laugh and cringe at the same time, I now know the answer. "Dylan..."

"You tell that boy I'll have you there at noon." She thanks the guy handing us our food and drinks at the last window, then pulls forward and does a quick check of the bag's contents before pulling away.

I can't help but appreciate her enthusiasm.

> Is noon okay? Dylan will bring me.

He sends three replies.

Yes!

> I can't wait. :)

Are you sure you're sure, though?

I grin.

> I'll see you tomorrow, Milo.

He sends one more text.

> See you there. :)

"What made you give it a chance?" The excitement is still there, but her tone tells me the question is serious.

"Lilah."

"Well, I'm glad for it, kiddo." She reaches over and squeezes my knee. "That boy makes you smile."

"He does." Of course, one arrives just in time to drive the point home.

We get back to the house and eat our lunch at the kitchen table, talking about work and Milo and how tomorrow might go.

"You almost done with that stack of books yet?" She stands and tosses the wrappers from our meal in the trash.

"I will be after tonight."

"I'll add that to our shopping list, then." She grabs the pad of paper and starts searching for a pen.

I laugh. "I can just pick some up next time I go into work, Dylan."

She gives up on the pen search and tosses the pad

back on the counter. "You'd think I'd know this or somethin'."

"Think we can go visit Mom for a bit?"

"Whenever you're ready, kiddo, just let me know."

"I'm ready."

We head to the hospital and I'm pleased to find that Micah's name is not the one written on the nurse's board in her room. One of the other regulars is listed instead–a sweet older woman who always remembers my name.

Everything looks the same as it always does. I can never decide if that's good or bad. Nothing changing means she isn't getting worse, but that also tells me there probably hasn't been much progress, either.

I lean over the bed and kiss Mom's forehead. "I did something big today." I pull one of the chairs close to her bed and take a seat. "I don't know how to feel about it yet, but I think you'll be happy."

What if it's happy enough news to wake her up?

"Do you remember the guy I told you about? Milo? I, uh... I asked him to go on a date with me." An awkward giggle escapes without my permission and I slap my hand over my mouth. The action makes me giggle more.

I compose myself and continue.

"I know. I know I said that dating wasn't in the

plans, but... I just... he makes me smile when not much else does right now. And we talk really easy. And he's funny. And really sweet. And cute. And... and I think you're really going to like him, Mom."

I trace my fingers along the lines inside her palm, that thing I know she hates.

I can feel the emotion starting to build up inside, but I'm determined not to cry–not after everything so good that has happened today.

I stretch her fingers out and lay my head on her palm and whisper, "I'm ready for you to wake up now."

Seventeen

"How do I look?" I stretch my arms out and turn in a circle for Dylan. I haven't really done much different from normal. I put on a little eyeliner and mascara and opted for a flowy top with my leggings rather than a t-shirt like I've been wearing. I haven't put this much effort into my appearance in so long, I almost feel like I should expect something to go wrong.

"Beautiful, kiddo," Dylan winks and hands me my purse. "You good to go, then?"

Am I? Why am I so nervous? It's just me and Milo hanging out again, right? The same as always. Just... with more feelings.

A real date.

"Yeah, I think I've got everything." I open my purse and look inside. "Do I have everything?"

"You're gonna be late if you keep second-guessing it."

I suck in a breath and run everything through my head one more time.

I haven't forgotten anything I need to take with me. Everything that needs to be turned off is off. Everything that needs to be unplugged is unplugged.

I take one more deep breath. "Okay."

We start to walk toward the door and I double-back, checking again that all the knobs on the stove and coffee maker are in the right position. "Yes, I'm ready. Let's go."

I hurry out the door before I can come up with any other reason to wait a little longer.

The ride to the mall feels like it takes forever. I can't stop fidgeting in my seat. Dylan notices. "You're gonna wring your fingers right off if you keep that up." She chuckles as I stop and adds, "Don't be nervous, kiddo. You're gonna have a great time."

"You don't think it's gonna be awkward?"

"Oh, you're damn sure it will be!" She laughs. "But you'll get over it and things will be just like they have been."

"We haven't been more than friends before this, though."

Dylan snorts but doesn't comment on that. She points to the building and says, "Isn't that your boy right there?" I follow her finger's direction and see that Milo is, indeed, standing by the main entrance to the mall. She chuckles and adds, "I swear if I didn't know that boy was always blushing over you, I'd think he has rosacea."

"Please don't tell him that."

"I'll keep it to myself, don't worry."

Dylan finds a spot to park and we head over to meet him there.

Milo's eyes light up when he sees us. "Hey!" He waves and asks, "I hope traffic wasn't too bad for you?"

"Nah, not for this time of day," Dylan says. That grin she always gets when I'm around Milo makes a show. "Well, you have my number if you need me. I'm gonna go check out the merchandise, okay?" She doesn't wait for a reply. She squeezes past us, giving Milo a slap on the shoulder as she goes.

He stumbles forward a step, mumbling to himself, "Why does everybody do that?"

I stare at my feet. There's a weird tingle in the air between us, and I can't bring myself to face it. We're the same people we were before I admitted I like him, right? Why is it so awkward, then?

"Are you hungry?" Milo finally breaks the silence I didn't want to face. "We could start walking toward the food court?"

"Yeah, that's–that sounds good." A nervous chuckle displays my embarrassment. Milo tries to bite a grin that I don't miss as we start walking that way.

"So, how has your day been so far?" he asks.

"Good." Just stressing out and second-guessing every step leading up to our date. "Yours?"

"Not bad. A little tired after helping my parents last night."

The tension slowly starts to ease as we fall into conversation like we're used to. "What were you helping your parents with? I mean, if you don't mind me asking."

"Yeah, it's fine." His eyes light up as he continues. "So, I just moved out and got my own place a few months ago, not long after I started at the shop, actually."

"Your own place?" I know Milo is a couple years older than me, but it's still surprising to think of him living on his own.

"Yeah, my parents rent out a few different places in

town and one of the tenants just moved out, so I asked them if I could rent it."

"That's pretty cool."

"Yeah. It's just a little place, but the rent is cheap and the landlords are nice." He grins.

"It helps that they're your parents."

"One thousand percent." Milo laughs. "But, yeah, so I moved out and Dad was wanting to turn my old room into a craft room for Mom so that he could finally have the garage to himself."

"Your parents sound cute." And really normal.

"They're so adorable it's disgusting."

"Did you get everything done last night?"

"Yeah, but it took forever. We didn't realize just how much stuff Mom had out there." He makes an exaggerated sigh. "I've never even seen her use any of the craft stuff. Buy it? Yes. She buys so much craft stuff. But I've never seen her use any of it." He shrugs.

"Maybe now she will?"

"After all that, I hope so."

Milo stops walking as we get to the food court. It's busy, but it usually is, especially at lunchtime. "What are you hungry for?" I ask.

"Do you like philly cheesesteak?"

I smile. "I love that place."

"Do you want to find somewhere to sit while I go grab us some philly sandwiches, then?"

"Are you trying to pay for my food again?"

He grins. "I absolutely am."

"Are you ever going to let me pay for things? I didn't even get to buy cotton candy at the zoo before–" I don't finish the sentence.

He holds up a hand. "You can buy dessert today."

"Fine. But the date isn't over until that happens." I called it a date. Out loud. To Milo.

"I'll accept your terms." He turns and heads off to get our lunch, leaving me shaking my head and praying he didn't notice the blush I'm sure I have.

There aren't a lot of options left for seating. I find a table on the far edge of the food court and claim it.

I text Milo so he knows.

> I'm over by the perfume place.

I watch him pull his phone out of his pocket and read my text. He looks up and scans the area, smiling and waving when he spots me.

There are a few people in line ahead of Milo, but they seem to be getting through it pretty fast. It's weird to think that I'm on a date with him. This is so far off from where I thought I'd be at this point in my life that it's almost comical. I know I've had to change my plans a few times, but I never expected "actual first date" to make it on the list for a while.

I glance up again. Milo is putting an obnoxious amount of ketchup packets onto the tray. He pauses a second before adding one more.

They hand him the last of our food and he heads back this way.

Setting the tray on the table, he says, "I wasn't sure how much ketchup we'd need so I just grabbed a bunch. I can get more if we need it."

"How much ketchup do you think I need for my fries, Milo?"

"You don't dip your sandwich in it?" he asks. I take my food, shaking my head. "Oh, you're missing out."

"What did you get me?" I pick up the sandwich and peek inside.

Milo picks his own up and grins. "Three cheese with bacon. I'll eat your bacon if you don't want it."

"I'll keep mine, thank you." He frowns and I can't help but laugh. "Were you hoping I'd give it to you?"

"Maybe." His face says everything.

"Well, this happens to be my favorite sandwich from there, and the bacon is the best part."

"Yeah?" His eyes light up again. I don't think it takes much to make Milo happy.

"Yes, Milo." The words come out on a giggle.

"Next time I'll get us extra bacon, then."

"Will you let me pay next time?"

"Not a chance."

We eat without much conversation. The tension that had mostly dissipated before makes it way back again as the silence settles between us.

Milo finishes his food before I do. "What really made you want to ask me out? As more than friends, I mean." There's a world of quiet wonder in his eyes.

I take the last bite of my sandwich as I think of how I want to reply.

Milo is quick to say, "You don't have to answer. I was just curious."

I shake my head as I swallow, setting my trash on the tray between us. "It was Lilah." I slowly look up at him, meeting his eyes.

"She was your best friend, right?" His voice is soft, but it still stings to hear him say "was".

I nod, surprising myself as I continue. "I went out and talked to her about everything... my feelings... you... my guilt over it all." I pause, searching his eyes for any indication that he's ready to run away from my crazy. He gives me nothing, so I go on. "I don't know. It's like I could hear her telling me to stop being stupid."

Milo is quiet for a long minute.

"I don't know what I can say to ease your guilt. But we can wait if you need more time, Ellessy." He reaches forward and gently places his hand on one of mine, almost as if asking permission. I don't pull away. "I do really like you. But I can be a friend if that's all you need right now."

My heart could melt and I'm pretty sure he'd catch it to pour back in later.

I gently trace circles around his knuckles with my free hand, much the same way I do with Mom when I visit her. "I know I'm still struggling with a lot of things. But you make me smile. And I want you to keep making me smile."

Milo flips his hand over and scoops both of mine up with both of his. "Then that's what I'm gonna do." He gives my hands a gentle squeeze before releasing them and getting up to get rid of our trash.

He comes back to the table with his hand held out and asks "Shall we?"

I smile and take his hand. "We shall."

We walk around the mall some more, falling back into conversation like we used to–playful and easy. The tension plaguing the day fades away and things feel... *normal*. It's the most normal I've felt in months.

I silently send a thank you up to Lilah for giving me the push I needed.

"Do you want to go to the arcade?" Milo asks, stopping near the entrance.

I haven't been to the arcade in what feels like forever. "Yeah, let's do it."

"What do you want to hit up first?"

"Skee-ball." I don't hesitate with my answer and it makes Milo laugh. "What?"

"You already knew the answer to that question, didn't you?"

I nod. "It's my favorite. Mom used to bring me and Lilah to play."

I pull my purse around and start rummaging for quarters. I empty the change into my hand and dump what I don't need back into my purse. "I've got... two dollars? No, Two twenty-five."

Milo pulls a twenty out of his wallet and walks over to the change machine. "We can do better than that." He wiggles his eyebrows as he wiggles the twenty in front of himself.

"No, you don't have to break a twenty just for arcade quarters, Milo."

He holds up a hand and inserts the bill into the machine. "I am making this adult decision for the both of us."

The arcade isn't very busy, but that's pretty normal. Most of the locals have spent plenty of time here and not many parents seem to want to mess with bringing their children in anymore. Thankfully, that means there isn't anyone hovering around the skee-ball machines. We claim the two closest to the far wall.

I put two quarters in my machine and grab the first ball. I toss it up the ramp and it falls in the middle hole for 40 points. Milo puts a couple quarters in his machine and says, "You ready to see a true master?"

I scoff and grab the next ball. "Show me what you've got, Trip."

He narrows his eyes and says, "Watch and learn, House Fire." Milo tosses the ball up the ramp. It lands in the bottom hole for 10 points.

I snort. "Am I learning humility?"

Milo hangs his head. "Yes. Yes, you are."

He isn't terrible at the game. We spend an hour and all of our quarters–plus another five dollars worth–on nothing but skee-ball. Milo gathers up all of our tickets after the last game and asks, "What incredibly mediocre prize do you want to get with all these?

I laugh. "Incredibly mediocre?"

"When was the last time you looked at what this many tickets can get you?"

"It's been a while," I admit. We walk over to the

counter and set our tickets down. The man behind it counts them while we look at our options. Milo isn't kidding. The tickets don't go very far anymore. But maybe they never did?

"You've got enough for anything on one of these shelves or in the case." The worker gestures to three shelves behind him and then the counter.

"So many choices." The sarcasm in Milo's voice isn't subtle enough for the worker to miss it. He grunts, obviously annoyed. I'm sure it's not the first time he's heard something like that.

I look over the options. The counter has a lot of little things like erasers and keychains and a couple of candies. The shelves have some small toys and trinkets and a couple of little stuffed animals. Nothing worth the almost thirty dollars we put into the games.

"I want that one." I point at the shelf with the little stuffed animals on it.

"Which one are we lookin' at?" The worker asks.

"The big rubber ducky on the far right." I point again. Behind the last stuffed animal is a bigger than normal rubber ducky.

He pulls it down and sets it on the counter. "You have enough to get one more thing out of here." He taps the top of the counter.

I look in the case and see that there are more

rubber duckies on the middle shelf, this time really small. Like something you'd see in a quarter machine. "Give me one of those tiny ducks to go with the big guy, please." I smile and turn to Milo. He has a big grin plastered to his face. "What?"

He shakes his head. "Nothing."

The guy behind the counter hands me my rubber ducks. "Thank you," I tell him. He just grunts and nods, sitting back down and looking at his phone.

I pull my duckies close and smile as we leave. "Do you like your incredibly mediocre prizes?"

"I will love him forever."

"Him? Just one of them?"

"Yeah, this one is for you." I hold the smaller duck out for Milo.

He puts his hand on his chest and pretends to be honored. "I will cherish him like he's worth twenty bucks."

I laugh. "You better."

My phone vibrates and I pull it out of my pocket. There's a text from Dylan asking how things are going.

"Is everything okay?"

"Yeah, it's just Dylan checking up on me." I glance at the time on my phone. "Wow, we've been here for a while."

Milo pulls his own phone out of his pocket and checks the time. "Has it really been three hours?"

"Time flies when you're having fun, right?" I smile up at him. I've never noticed just how much taller than me he is.

"That's what they say." He returns the smile. "I think they're right."

"Maybe." I sigh, realizing that my left leg is starting to limp a little harder.

"Do we need to start walking back to the entrance?" Milo asks, gesturing in that direction.

"Yeah, I think we do." I rub my left thigh. "I think my leg is kind of done with the day." I can feel my embarrassment starting to sneak in.

Milo puffs up his chest. "Do you need me to carry you?"

I laugh. "No, Milo. You are not carrying me through the mall."

He shrugs. "The offer is open."

I shake my head and send Dylan a text to let her know we'll meet her at the entrance. She sends a reply saying she'll be there.

"So... today was really fun." Milo's cheeks turn red, but he keeps talking. "I mean I had a really good time with you today. And, uh, I'd really like to hang out again sometime soon. If... if that sounds good to you?"

"You know you'll see me at work, right?"

His blush gets brighter. "Yeah, I know. But…" He shrugs and rakes his hand through his hair as we stop near the entrance. "You know."

"I know what you mean, Milo."

Dylan is already waiting by the door. I wonder how close she was? I picture her sprinting from the other side of the mall.

She waves at us, but doesn't move.

Milo holds out his hand. I bite back a giggle and reach out to accept his handshake. "It was nice having a date with you, Ellessy."

If you told me I was melting, I might just believe you. "I had a nice date with you, too, Milo."

He takes his hand back and holds his new tiny duck up with the other. "Thanks for the prize."

I hold mine up. "I should be thanking you."

He grins and glances over to Dylan, waving. Looking back to me, he says, "See you later, Lowercase."

Of all the nicknames he's given me, that's the one that makes me smile the most. "See you soon."

I turn and walk over to Dylan.

"Did the date go well?" She asks as we start walking to the SUV.

"It did." I don't even try to hide my smile this time. "It really did."

Eighteen

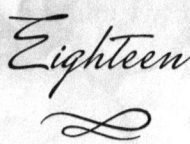

"I'll message you when I'm ready to come home, but I'm determined to make it through an entire shift today," I tell Dylan as I open the door to the SUV and get out.

"Just let me know. I'll—"

"Go home." I close the door and smile. "You don't need to hang around nearby all day when home isn't that far. I'll be fine."

She stares at me a moment before giving in, driving off in the direction of the house. I'm happy that she's actually going home and trusting me with this.

I turn back toward the shop and make my way to the door, nervous tingles of excitement pushing me forward. I'm working with Milo, of course. It's also our first time seeing each other since our date a few days ago.

He isn't holding the door open for me like he usually does–not that I mind. Judging by the cars in the parking lot, I'm guessing that it's already busy. Walking in, I can see my guess is right. I head into the back and get signed in on the timesheet so I can start helping Milo right away.

I go over to the register where Milo is finishing up a transaction with a customer. "How about I take over here and you can walk the floor?" I ask him. I briefly think about how lame it is that those are the first words he hears in person from me since our date.

He must not have noticed me when I came in. His face is immediately enveloped with a smile that his eyes reflect. "Good thinking," he says.

He hands the customer their change and books, and moves so that I can take his place at the register.

Milo easily glides onto the sales floor and starts helping customers with finding their books and giving recommendations for ones they didn't even realize they wanted. It isn't a very big shop, so there's only one register. With me getting customers taken care of there and Milo on the floor, we're mostly able to keep things running smooth.

Most of the customers are regulars. Conversations at the register run a little longer than usual, with many of them asking me how I am and saying how happy they've been to see me back at work again. Even with that, I'm able to keep up with the small line.

It stays consistently busy like that for a few hours before the crowd dissipates and Milo and I are the only ones left in the store.

Milo shoves his hands in his back pockets and steps over to me in that awkward way that he always sort of is. "Hey..."

I can't help but smile. "Hey."

"So... I know I asked you the other day, but I... I just want to make sure—"

"Don't you ask me again, Milo." I laugh, knowing immediately that he's referring to him asking me on another date. "Just accept that I like you."

He holds up his hands. "Okay. I just didn't want you to feel pressured or anything." He dramatically runs a hand through his hair. "I know how charming I can be."

I roll my eyes. "Ah, yes. That's what did it. Your charm is so intense, it's amazing there's still this much distance between us right now." I raise an eyebrow at him to seal my sarcasm.

"I mean, I can fix that." He steps forward.

I laugh and I'm the one holding up my hands this time. He stops. "Thank you, though. My Mom has taught me enough about men to know that they don't always care about stuff like that. So," I take a deep breath and smile. "Thank you."

Milo opens his mouth to say something, but a customer comes into the store. He grins and turns away to help them instead. More customers follow and we pick back up with the busy pace from earlier.

It feels like every person that comes through stares at me with such a strange mix of excitement and pity–like they're so happy to see me back, but burdened with the knowledge of why I was gone.

I can feel the anxiety fogging my mind. I smile and nod and only half pay attention to their attempts at conversation, willing my brain to follow a trick from the internet and count by fours long enough to forget about having a panic attack.

Not this time. Not today.

I keep counting in my mind and working through the customer line until the last one comes through and I realize it's time to close. Milo walks them to the door and locks it behind them.

I breathe. A long, deep breath that feels like it fills my entire body. Closing my eyes, I run through a few more numbers, just long enough for that feeling in my chest to go away.

"Are you okay?" Milo is standing a few feet away when I open my eyes, with that same concerned look he had at the zoo.

"Yeah, I'm fine." I raise my arms up and stretch, my back audibly popping as I do.

"Do you need a water or anything?"

I shake my head. "No, I'm okay." I stand and change the subject. "It's been a while since I've closed. You want to take lead?"

"Oh, you don't have to stay and close, I can do everything if you want to head home."

"I'm already here and it was a busy day. I'm staying. Just tell me where you want me to start."

Milo grins, clearly not upset that I've chosen to stay. "If you want to start putting these back," He hands me the books that customers decided not to buy at the register. "I can count down the drawer?"

"I'm on it." I take the stack of books from him and set to putting them back in their places on the shelves, doing my best to tidy things as I go.

"It was pretty busy today," I say.

Milo finishes counting the money in his hand before he replies. "Yeah, I have no clue what that was about."

"It might be something to do with the weather?" I offer. It's been a really nice day, so it would make sense for more people to be out shopping and enjoying it.

"Maybe it was me? I did mention how charming I am."

I roll my eyes. He can't see me do it, but he laughs like he did. I peek around the shelf and see he's still quietly laughing to himself as he finishes counting the drawer down.

Shaking my head, I get back to putting the last few books away.

"I'm heading back to put the drawer in the safe. You sure you don't want a water while I'm back there?" I step around the bookcase and see Milo standing at the door to the back of the shop.

"No, I'm fine. Is there anything else that needs done or should I focus on the shelves?"

"You can go ahead and start on that. The only other thing is sweeping, so I'll grab the broom on my way back."

"Okay."

I turn back to the shelves and start straightening the books and making sure that they're all in their right places. It's always been amazing to me how many customers pick things up from one shelf and put them back on a different one when they change their mind.

Even our regulars do it. I guess when you don't work retail, these things just don't occur to you.

Milo comes back with the broom and sweeps the store as I get everything else straightened up, talking while we work. I still can't get over how easy things are with him.

"I can't wait for my mom to meet you." I realize what I said a moment after the words leave my mouth, but they aren't any less true.

Milo stops sweeping. "You want me to meet her?"

I give him a side glance. "No, Milo, I'm going to date you in secret." His face turns red and I can't help but giggle. "Of course I want you to meet her."

He smiles and goes back to sweeping. "I can't wait to meet her, too." He gets quiet and adds, "I hope she wakes up soon, Ellessy."

"So do I." I look up at the ceiling, begging the tears I can feel coming on to slide back down and stay inside. "You know," I clear my throat and look at Milo. "You could come with me to visit her sometime. If you wanted."

He stops sweeping again and stares at me for a long moment, as if trying to see if I meant what I said. "Is that what you want?"

Is it? "I think it might be nice."

Milo starts to grin but gets a horrified look on his

face. "I would be meeting your mom before she meets me. You're setting me up for failure, House Fire."

"Oh, God, I didn't even think about that." I shake my head. "Okay, maybe we should hold off."

"Well, she's going to wake up before we have to think about that anyway." He looks at me a moment longer–not a hint of doubt on his face–and gets back to work.

As busy as we were today, it doesn't take too long to get the store looking ready for open tomorrow. Milo finishes sweeping and helps me get the rest of the closing tasks done. We chat about poetry while we finish up, and the time feels like it flies by.

"Are you ready to clock out?" Milo asks, holding the door to the back open.

"Yeah, I think we got everything." I go through the door and over to the time sheet.

I can feel Milo close to me as I write in my time. I turn to hand him the pencil, our fingers touching as he takes it. Tingles shoot through me and I linger, not letting go.

I look up at him. He's at least a foot taller than me. He leans in slowly, giving me every chance to back away, but it feels like it happens so fast. I close my eyes and lean into his kiss.

They say in fairy tales that a first kiss feels magical.

If those kisses feel anything like this, I understand the sentiment.

I struggle to keep the guilt from ruining it.

He pulls away. "I'm sorry, I–" Milo has blushed a lot since I've met him, but I don't think his face has ever been this red.

"No, it's, um… that was…" I'm at a loss for words, so I just smile. I can hear Dylan's voice in my head. *If awkward was made outta butter, y'all would be melted.*

"Would it be okay if I did that again?"

I don't hesitate. "Yes."

He cups my face with his hands and pulls me in for another kiss, just as soft and gentle as the first. He lingers a few moments longer this time, resting his forehead against mine when he finally pulls his lips away. I reach up and slide my fingers over his, keeping my eyes closed and letting the moment take me over.

I feel him start to pull away, so I open my eyes and take a step back. Milo's face is still red, but he has a grin I can't help but match. "I, uh…" He clears his throat and turns to the timesheet. "What time did you clock out? I'll," he clears his throat again. "I'll put that, too."

He writes in his time and we make our way out to the front door. Milo fumbles with his key, but manages to get the building locked behind us.

In all the excitement, I forgot to text Dylan. I send

her a message letting her know that I'm ready for her to pick me up.

"Do you need a ride home?" Milo asks, looking around the empty parking lot. There's only one vehicle–a truck–that I'm assuming is his.

I shake my head. "No, Dylan is on the way. But, thank you."

"We can sit in my truck while we wait for her if you want?"

"You don't have to wait with me."

"I want to."

"Thanks," I mumble. I'm growing more and more attached to his smiles with every one he gives me.

"Oh! I almost forgot." He runs over to his truck and opens the door, leaning in and grabbing something. He comes back with a book in his hand. "Here."

"What's this?" I take it from him and read the cover.

"It's one of my favorite poetry books. I thought you might like to read it."

"Thank you. I was actually needing something new to read."

"Let me know what you think."

"I will." The air is practically dripping awkward energy.

Dylan pulls in and stops right in front of us. She

waves and Milo waves back. "Well, I guess I'll see you soon?" I can tell he hopes it's really soon.

I do, too. "Definitely." I smile and start to walk away.

Milo runs over to his truck and waves one more time before he gets in. I shake my head and wave back as I get into the SUV with Dylan.

She has her classic "I can sense something is up but I'm not going to ask about it" look on her face. "Did you have a good shift?"

If she had any doubt that her senses were right, my grin gives it away. "I'll tell you all about it when we get home."

She smiles. "You hungry?"

I nod. "I haven't really eaten since before work."

"Good, 'cause I have dinner ready at home."

"I can't wait."

"Me either, kiddo." She laughs. "I have a feelin' you've got something particularly good to tell me."

"I just might."

We get home and Dylan wastes no time asking what the news is as we sit down to eat. I tell her all about how my shift went, leaving out no details.

I'm pretty sure she could win a world record for the grin she gets when I tell her about our kiss. "Who knew that boy was hidin' so much smooth behind all that red face embarrassment?"

We finish up dinner and I head back to my room to read the book Milo gave me. I fall asleep with it still in my hand.

For the first time in months, I don't have any nightmares.

Nineteen

"Hello?" I pull myself from my nap, answering the phone without looking to see who it might be.

Maybe it's Milo? I grin at the idea, stretching as I wait for his response.

"Is this Ellessy Porter?" It's not Milo. The voice sounds familiar but I can't really place it.

"Yes, who is this?"

"Ellessy, this is Micah at Rook County Hospital. I'm your mom's nurse." I sit up, fully awake, excitement shooting through my veins.

I did know that voice. It's Mom's nurse, the one I don't like. And if he's calling me, that can only mean something big.

Is this it? Did she finally wake up? Am I going to get to talk to my mom again?

I try to stay calm as I ask, "Is everything okay? Did she wake up?"

There's a pause before he speaks again. "I'm afraid not, Miss Porter." My entire body goes cold almost immediately, tingling at the base of my neck and dripping down my spine. "It would be best if you came to the hospital right away."

I'm not even sure if I say anything. Everything sounds too loud, my head feels too big. I'm vaguely aware of walking out of my room and into the kitchen. I mumble to Dylan that the hospital called and we have to leave. She jumps up and grabs her keys without a word.

It feels like I'm floating, a balloon being directed by Dylan. I don't remember getting in the SUV. I don't remember the drive to the hospital. I don't remember the journey to her floor.

But my focus is sharp when we get up to her room. Micah is standing next to Mom's bed, speaking to her doctor. They abruptly stop their conversation and turn to me with pity on their faces.

"Miss Porter," the doctor says. "I'm Doctor Livingston. I've been part of the team taking care of your mother." He offers a smile, but it's empty, one that he's given to a thousand patients when he's had to tell them something they don't want to hear.

"What's going on?" Dylan asks. "And don't sugar-coat it." I don't know if it's the nurse inside her wanting him to cut to the chase, or the blood we share making her want answers, but I'm glad for either one.

Dr. Livingston and Nurse Micah trade glances. "Mrs. Porter's organs–"

"Ms," I correct him, more stalling than anything. I know more than ever that I'm not ready to hear what he has to say.

He stops and clears his throat, trading another glance with Micah before correcting himself. "Ms. Porter's organs have started failing. Her vital signs and labs have started to decline," Dr. Livingston looks at Dylan who gives him a short nod before he continues, "and we don't expect her to make it through the night."

Everything feels like it's trying to crash down around me while I use all of my strength to hold it above my head. This can't be right. Mom can't be dying. She has to make it. I *need* her to make it.

"Do you understand, Miss Porter?" Micah asks, as if I'm a child who can't comprehend what's happening. My anger for him intensifies.

I ignore him and look at Dr. Livingston. "There's a

chance, though, right? There's a chance she might pull through?" I'll cling to whatever hope they give me. I'm not giving up.

"Kiddo..." Dylan's voice is soft and quiet for the first time I can remember since Lilah's funeral.

I hold my hands out in front of me, shaking my head like I'm trying to shake their words out of it. "She has a chance, right?" The desperation in my voice doesn't even try to hide itself.

Dr. Livingston also doesn't hide anything in his own voice. "Miss Porter, the chances are very slim."

"But they're still there?" I have to hang onto something, even if it's slim.

"Why don't you go sit by your mama, Ellessy?" Dylan squeezes my shoulders and gently urges me toward the bed. I don't fight it. I go right over and kiss Mom on the forehead like I always do when I come visit.

God, I should've visited more.

I pull up a chair and scoot it as close to Mom's bed as I can manage. I slide my hand into hers and lay my head across it. Maybe if my tears touch her skin, she'll wake up like in the books? Maybe if I kiss her hand, my love will heal her?

I can hear Dylan talking to Dr. Livingston behind me. They're far enough back and talking quietly enough that I can't make out what they're saying. But I don't need to. My gut tells me it's nothing I want to hear, anyway.

Mom has to make it. There's no way around that, she just has to. I know my plans keep getting messed up and changing, but none of them involve a world without her in it. I don't know how to plan for that and I won't do it. I refuse.

Mom *is* going to wake up.

I already lost Lilah.

I can't lose her, too.

"Hey, kiddo..." Dylan says, startling me from my thoughts as she squats down beside me. "Who do you want me to call?" Her voice is so soft and gentle, unlike the flavorful boom I'm so used to.

"I don't know." Who do we have to call? Before Dylan came into my life, it was pretty much just me, Mom, and Lilah. Can you make a call to Heaven and tell them now isn't the time?

I can feel the ache in my chest as the words rush from my mouth. "She's going to wake up, anyway, Dylan. So we don't need to call anyone. They can talk to her when she wakes up, alright?"

Dylan squeezes my shoulder again and stands. "I'll give Abbie a call, okay?"

I nod and turn back to Mom. Abbie would want

to know what's going on. And she can tell Rob and Martha and Milo where I am if it takes a while for Mom to get better.

Milo.

I pull my phone out of my pocket and see I've missed a few texts from him. I reread them three times, but my brain won't process what they say.

I send him a simple reply.

> I'm at the hospital. Mom's organs are failing. I can't really talk.

I don't know why I'm so blunt. I want to say something more, something better, but my mind is chaos right now.

His reply is fast, like always.

> Oh God I'm so sorry Ellessy. Call me if you need anything. Call me when you know something. I'm here.

I put my phone back in my pocket.

Yesterday, his words made my chest tingle. Yesterday, we kissed. I had my *first* kiss.

And today...

Today, I'm begging my mom to stay alive.

I glance up at the monitors that show her heart

rate and other things I don't understand. The numbers keep dropping. I know enough to know that's not what we want.

"You have to wake up, Mom." I squeeze her hand with both of mine. Maybe if I squeeze hard enough, she'll wake up and tell me that it hurts? Tell me she's here now and I can stop? "You have to meet this boy I've been telling you about. And I need you to wake up and argue with me about Dylan, okay? I'm ready to have that conversation now, okay?" I shake her hand as if it'll shake her back to me. "I need you to wake up and be my mom, again.

"I've been pushing with everything I have to get better, Mom, for both of us. Have I not been pushing hard enough?" The tears flow faster and I squeeze my eyes tight, pulling Mom's hand closer to my face. "I can push harder, Mom. Just tell me. Just tell me what I need to do."

I hear movement behind me. It sounded like someone entered the room, but I don't care to turn and look. Dylan speaks to them quietly, and the reply sounds like Abbie.

Hands gently slide over my shoulders and pull me into an embrace from behind. "Hey, Ellie," Abbie whispers.

She lets go and moves around to stand closer to

Mom. She smiles at me, but I can see the pain behind it.

"Hey" is all I can say.

Abbie leans over and whispers something to Mom. I can't catch what she says, but it makes me feel some sort of good knowing that I'm not the only one who talks to her. She brushes some hair from Mom's forehead and plants a kiss there, whispering something more before she pulls away.

Her eyes are watery when she turns back to me. "You just give me a call if you need anything, okay? Don't worry about work or any of that right now, I'll talk to Rob and Martha. Just focus on you and your Mama, okay?" I nod and give her as much of a smile as I can manage. It doesn't feel real, but something tells me she gets it. Abbie kneels next to me and leans forward to give me another hug, holding just a little longer this time.

She stands up and kisses me on the top of my head before adding, "You and Dylan both have my number. Don't hesitate to use it."

Abbie walks back to Dylan and I hear her ask how Mom is doing. I tune out Dylan's reply. Mom is going to be okay. I don't care how things look right now. She's going to be just fine.

I close my eyes and lay my head across her hand,

willing my energy to flow into her and make everything all right.

I don't know how much time passes. Dylan tries to get me to eat, but the idea makes me want to vomit. Dr. Livingston and Nurse Micah ask me what feels like a million times if I want to consider withdrawing support–to just let her die–as her vitals continue to drop. I tell them each time that I refuse to give up on her–that if there is even a tiny chance that she will make it, I'm not letting go.

I'm thankful when the shift change comes and Micah finally leaves, replaced by one of the other nurses I actually like.

Still, the numbers on the screen keep dropping as the night goes on, and my hope starts dropping with them.

I say it over and over to myself, *she has to make it*. My mind can't even imagine a life without her. Especially after losing Lilah, I don't know how I can make it without Mom, too.

I don't know how to plan for this. I don't know if I *can*.

I fall asleep holding Mom's hand, lost in troubled thought, having gone without rest for more than twenty-four hours.

The side of my face is sticky from crying when I

wake up. Dylan is standing beside me and Mom's nurse is on the other side of the bed. Looking at the monitor, I can see that her pulse is still going, but those numbers are so low it makes my stomach drop.

I stand and lift Mom's hand, bringing it to my face. I notice the stiffness in her fingers as I try to cup my cheek with it.

"Dylan..." Her name sputters from my lips on a choked cry. I look up at her through the tears blinding my eyes.

Dylan gently takes Mom's hand and sets it back down. She wraps her arm around me and pulls me close. "I know, kiddo."

I don't have time to process it. The numbers keep dropping until the line on her screen goes flat. I scream, but I can't hear it. I'm crying, but no sound fills my head besides that beep. My legs give out and Dylan holds me up.

This can't be happening. I can't lose my Mom. She can't be–

The monitor comes back to life with a heartbeat, and my hope comes crashing back in just long enough to give me pause.

The nurse tells me it's a hiccup. That the medicine in her body can sometimes make the heart beat after she's already passed.

My world falls apart all over again, feeling like I've lost her twice.

There's no more hope to cling to. She didn't make it.

Mom's really gone.

Twenty

Time passes like it's moving without me. It feels like I'm living the first days after the car accident all over again.

Only this time, it's Mom in the casket and not Lilah.

The funeral is a blur. It seems like hundreds of people are there. I don't know how many of them actually knew Mom and how many are just people who've been following our story since the benefit auction, but person after person walks by to shake my hand and offer their sympathies as they go to view Mom in the casket. I feel so empty standing here, and the pain floods me like water from a popped balloon as they lower her into her final resting place at the cemetery.

Her *final* resting place. Because she doesn't get to come back home.

I lie in bed for days–weeks–ignoring the world. I've lost sense of time, letting the pain consume me–filling every inch of my body like a cold, thick liquid I can't escape.

Life sucks and everybody dies.

Everyone but me.

Why wasn't it me?

I wish so much that there was a physical reason for the pain I feel right now. A gaping wound or deep injury–something I can see and bandage and tend to. Something other than my stupid, broken heart.

It's as if it's made of glass and falling apart–the shattered pieces tearing up the rest of my insides as they break away and hit everything on the way down.

How am I supposed to live like this? I'm useless. I don't even know if I *want* to be alive anymore.

My best friend is dead. Mom is dead. I've pushed everyone away and hidden myself in my room for so long, I have no clue who I still have left. "Alone" doesn't begin to cover how I feel.

Even with Dylan here. She moved in permanently a few days after Mom died. No matter how much I've kept to myself and ignored her, she's been there for me, uprooting her entire life and taking care of everything. She set up the funeral, she got Mom a plot at the cemetery, she's taken care of any bit of paperwork and bills and all of the things I couldn't even get my mind to think about. I have so much to thank Dylan for, not the least that she gave up whatever might have been waiting for her back home in Illinois, just to take care of me when I've been so distant.

And then there's Milo.

I've pushed him away the most. I haven't looked at my phone since the hospital. I know Dylan called him because he was at the funeral. He's stopped by the house a few times, but I didn't even leave my room.

I can't tell if I feel more guilty for treating him like this or for the feelings I still have for him when I should be grieving Mom.

I roll over and see Dylan leaning against my doorway.

"Get up, kiddo, we've got somewhere to go today." Her voice is gentle but the words are firm.

"I don't feel like going anywhere." My own voice sounds rusty, like I've forgotten how to use it.

"I know you don't. But it's non-negotiable this time." She comes over and pulls the blanket off of me. "Get up. Go get your stinky ass in the shower and put some clean clothes on." She holds her hand out to help me up. "Come on, you'll feel better once that water hits ya, I promise."

Where does she want to go that needs me to come with her? Dylan has been doing everything without me lately. She hasn't once pressured me to go when I've told her I didn't want to, and I haven't wanted to go anywhere since–

Curiosity spills into my darkness. I take her hand and she pulls me up to stand.

Dylan opens the drawers on my dresser and pulls out some clothes. "Here, somethin' comfy." She hands them to me and gives me a gentle push through the door. "Now go get you a shower."

It's clear there's no getting out of today's trip.

My curiosity piques just a little more.

I set my clothes down in the bathroom and grab a towel, suddenly realizing that I can't remember the last time I took a shower. Have I taken one since the fu– since I've been home? Have I even changed my clothes? I sniff my shirt and immediately regret it.

I peel off my clothes and toss them in the hamper. I really don't want to look at myself, so I just get the water started and run a brush through my hair without using the mirror. Judging by the matting I have to fight through, it was a smart idea. The picture in my head can't be better than what I've let myself get to.

I step into the shower, closing my eyes and tilting my head back, moving directly under the stream. The water hits me like a warm slap to the face and my first night home after the accident comes to mind.

The water runs cold before I finally get out.

I throw on my clothes and pull the brush through my hair again, throwing it in a bun on top of my head rather than wasting time with the blow dryer–not caring that it's October and the wind will probably be cold.

I make the mistake of peeking in the mirror. I'm pretty sure I've lost ten pounds and the bags under my eyes aren't hiding anything. If I look like this now, how much worse did I look before my shower?

Dylan is waiting at the kitchen table. "Get your shoes on and grab whatever you need." She stands and moves over to the door, not commenting on my wet hair. Whatever this is, it must be important.

My curiosity grows more as Dylan drives. Where are we going? Why did I have to come?

Dylan doesn't sing along to the radio or even turn it on. She keeps her eyes on the road and her face a stone wall, giving nothing away.

Glancing out the window, it suddenly occurs to me where we're heading. The arch reading "Glass Hill" passes over us as Dylan pulls into the cemetery and parks.

She shuts the SUV off but doesn't get out or remove her seatbelt. I can feel the anxiety crawling up my chest as we sit here in silence.

This isn't somewhere I want to be.

Dylan shifts so that she's turned toward me a little. "You don't have to get out," she says.

"What are we doing here?"

"Just listen to me for a minute." She holds up a hand to keep me from saying anything else. "You've been layin' in your bed, ignoring the world for weeks. Now, I am not your mom, and I would never try to be her. But I know she would hop down from the heavens and hate me more than she already did if I let you keep livin' like this.

"I'm not askin' you to stop grieving, Ellessy. You ain't ever gonna stop that. But you do have to learn to live with that grief."

Dylan pauses a moment to clear her throat. "Listen, kiddo, there's a darkness that people lose themselves to. I've seen it many times in patients. For some it's hate. Or greed. Or addiction like your father." She leans over and grabs my hand, giving it a firm squeeze. "Your mother would never forgive me if I stood by and watched you lose yourself to that darkness, too."

Dylan's words hit me like a punch to the gut.

Am I going down a path like my father? I don't want to be like him. Not even a little bit.

"Baby steps are fine, kiddo," Dylan adds, giving my hand another squeeze. "It ain't easy and it doesn't happen overnight. But you can't make a step if you don't start movin'."

I stare at her hand on mine for a long time. My voice is quiet when I finally speak. "You're right."

I don't know what else to say but that. She *is* right. I've barely been living, wrestling with the wish that it was me who died and the guilt of knowing it would mean Mom and Lilah would be here with this pain instead.

I pull my hand away from Dylan's grasp and unbuckle my seatbelt. I pause to glance Dylan's way before I hop out. She gives me an encouraging smile, but I can sense the sadness behind it.

I feel a little more guilt tug at my heart, knowing her grief is felt for me.

I haven't been to the cemetery since Mom's funeral, but I know her grave is past the tree near Lilah's.

I stop by Lilah's headstone on the way, kissing my fingers and pressing the kiss to her stone.

Mom's grave is off by itself, past the edge of the

pond. Dylan took care of all the hard stuff, but I remember picking the headstone. It's such a weird thing to hang onto. Why is it I can't remember what day of the week we buried her on or the clothes we buried her in, but I know I picked out a headstone with a cardinal etched into it?

I kneel down in front of the stone and trace my fingers along her name. Lina Dominique Porter. The tears come without hesitation.

"Hey, Mom." My voice cracks. I shake my head to give myself a chance to wake up from this nightmare, but nothing happens.

I swallow back the urge to scream.

"I'm sorry I didn't come sooner. I, uh..." I tilt my head back, begging the tears not to come. "I haven't been doing so well, Mom."

My head starts to hurt. I don't know if it's from the grief itself, or from trying to hold it in.

A cry sputters out as I blurt, "I'm sorry, Mom. I'm so sorry." I lean forward and cry into my knees. "You weren't supposed to die. Not yet. Not like this. I–I should've visited more, pushed you harder when I talked to you, told you how much I needed you to wake up...

"Oh, Mom, I don't know how I'm supposed to live without you."

I curl up in the fetal position in front of her headstone and cry, soul-shaking sobs that have me biting my knee for solace–not stopping until the wind is what's making me shiver and the birds are the only creatures wailing.

I wipe the tears from my face and pull myself back up to a sitting position. "Dylan's right, isn't she?" I look out over the water and take a deep breath, trying to ignore the emotion fighting its way back up again. "I know I haven't been myself since you–Honestly, I haven't been myself since Lilah–"

I give a quick, frustrated sigh. I hate saying the word.

"I've been trying so hard to get that back, that normal we used to know. And I don't know how I can do that without you. Nothing is normal with you gone, with both of you gone. And I–I don't think I can do it. I don't know how."

Two cardinals fly past me and stop to rest on a headstone nearby. *Cardinals*. I look at the one etched into Mom's headstone.

Your mother would never forgive me if I stood by and watched you lose yourself to that darkness, too.

Dylan's voice rings through my head as I see the birds fly off over the pond, continuing on with life as though nothing has changed.

Laughter to my left draws my attention. A couple and their kids are visiting a grave nearby. The children lay a wreath of flowers over the corner of the headstone and giggle some more, singing the words, "Pre-tty for Grand-ma!" as they do. The parents hush them, but they have smiles to match their children's mood.

Life goes on.

A pang of jealousy hits me. How long before I can smile when I'm here? How long before I can find a normal like those people seem to have?

You do have to learn to live with that grief. It ain't easy and it doesn't happen overnight.

Dylan enters my mind again, frustrating me even more. How do I learn to live with it when it's tearing me apart?

Mom's voice hits me this time, as clear as if she were right here with me.

You plan what you can and leave wiggle room for the rest of it.

Her words flip a lightswitch in the darkness.

I haven't left any wiggle room. I shut myself in a room with my plans and stayed there when it caught fire.

How can I learn to live with my grief when I won't get out of the fire?

"Thanks, Mom," I whisper. I press another kiss to

my fingers and push this one onto Mom's headstone, accidentally bumping the calla lillies in the vase next to it. I adjust them, the texture not what I was expecting.

They're fake. Dylan must have brought them out here.

Warmth fills my chest. I almost smile.

I turn and head back to the SUV. Dylan sets her crossword book down as I climb in. "How did it go?" I can tell by her tone that she really wants to know if I'm okay. I'm thankful for the sentiment as much as I'm thankful she didn't actually say the words.

"Thank you for putting the flowers out. And for making sure they're fake ones."

Dylan smiles and shakes her head. "That wasn't me, kiddo."

I tilt my own head to the side, scrunching my eyebrows together. "Who was it?"

"That was all your boy."

"Milo brought them out here?"

She nods. "He did."

Milo's been out to see Mom. I don't know if I should feel good that he brought her flowers or ashamed that he came to visit her before I did.

"How did he know to get fake ones?"

"I might have mentioned that much. But the rest was on him."

More guilt snakes its way into my gut, if that's even possible at this point. I've barely spoken to Milo since the funeral. He's texted me, but I haven't answered. He's stopped by, but I stayed in my room and stared at the wall like he wasn't really there.

I've been awful to Milo.

And he's been putting flowers on my mother's grave.

I shake my head.

I want to smile again. I want to make plans again. And go to work. And not hide away in my room and lose myself to darkness.

I glance in the direction of Mom's grave and send another silent thank you her way.

Plan for what you can and leave wiggle room for the rest.

Well, I plan to focus on the good things in my life right now and worry about the rest later. I can do that. I can ignore the rest. I can shut it all away. Lock *it* in the room with the fire, not me.

"Hey, do you think you could make one of Mom's recipes tonight?" I look at Dylan and muster up as much of a smile as I can manage. Baby steps.

Her face lights up a little. "We sure can, kiddo." She starts the SUV and pulls away from the cemetery. "There's one in her book I've been wantin' to try. We'll swing by the store and grab what we're missin' to make it."

"And muffins, too."

"The way you've been eating, I'd make you a whole cake if you asked for it."

"Maybe tomorrow," I joke, managing a little more of a grin this time.

Dylan laughs and turns the radio up, singing along as she drives. It's nice to see her back to her old self. I'm hoping this new plan will get me back, too.

Twenty-One

I pull out my phone and press the little icon for texts. Milo's name is at the top of the short list of message threads, and I open our conversation.

Sliding through the texts he never fails to send me, my stomach does an uncomfortable flip. I've tried so hard to push him away. I've ignored him–both his messages and the times he's come over only to end up hanging out with Dylan while I stayed in bed.

I've been awful to Milo and he's kept coming back.

I really don't deserve his friendship, let alone anything more.

I swallow the guilt and send him a text.

> Hey

Just like before, I get a reply almost immediately.

> Hey! I'm so happy to hear from you!

Same old Milo.
I try to be the same old me.

> Do you want to hang out with me today?

I hope he isn't working.

> Yeah! Definitely. When do you want me to come over?

I can't believe it. I haven't completely pushed him away. He's put up with so much, but he hasn't decided he's done with me.

He really is too good to be true.

> I was hoping we could go out somewhere. The park maybe?

I don't get an immediate response this time. His hesitation makes me nervous.

Does he not want to go out? Maybe I did do more damage than I thought...

I send another text.

> I was hoping to get out of the house. I feel like I've been stuck here too long lol

It feels weird typing "lol". It's always a joke that people aren't really laughing out loud when they type that, but I don't think I'm laughing on the inside, either.

> Yeah that's fine. Which park were you thinking?

> The one on the square has a walking path. I'm ready now if you want to meet me there?

Yeah!

I get out of bed and change into something a little nicer, but good for a walk. My phone vibrates as I'm slipping my shoes on. It's Milo again.

> I'll see you there!

A mixture of anxiety and warmth fills my chest. I do my best to ignore the anxiety and focus on that warm feeling.

Focus on the good. Ignore the rest.

Dylan is sitting at the kitchen table with papers

spread out in front of her. Her eyebrows fly up when she sees me.

"If my eyes ain't playin' tricks, there she is." She gives me a warm grin that stretches ear to ear.

I force a smile, ignoring how uncomfortable it still makes me. "Milo is meeting me at the park on the square, if you'll give me a ride?" I catch concern in Dylan's expression. I don't give her a chance to voice it. "I thought a walk would be nice, so I asked if he wanted to hang out... baby steps, right?"

She stares at me for what feels like a long time before saying, "Milo's at the top of that list, ain't he?"

I nod. "He is."

Dylan stands up and tells me, "Grab a jacket and whatever else you need and let's get movin'. Don't want him waiting there all day. You and I both know he would."

We get in the SUV and Dylan turns the radio down. "You planning on puttin' that seatbelt on?"

"Oh. Yeah, I almost forgot." To be honest, it wasn't exactly a priority.

Dylan waits until I'm buckled before she pulls out of the driveway.

"Which park are we headin' to?"

"The one on the square downtown." I point in that direction. She changes lanes.

"So this new plan of yours," Dylan turns the radio down so that the music is barely loud enough to hear. "What's it all about?"

I pretend there isn't anxiety fighting its way into the picture. I start squeezing the tips of my fingers, hoping that might distract me from it. "Hmm?"

"You've got some kind of plan cookin' up there, kiddo. You always do."

She knows me too well. I shrug, more a fidgety movement than an actual shrug. "Mom said something to me once that I remembered when we were there yesterday."

"Yeah? What's that?"

"Plan for what you can and leave wiggle room for the rest of it."

"Smart woman."

"The smartest woman I know. Knew." I clear my throat.

"Mmhmm." Dylan nods. "Now explain it like I'm confused as a chicken who got mittens for Christmas."

One corner of my mouth turns up. I love her way with phrases. "I'm just going to focus on the good things and worry about the rest later."

Dylan keeps her eyes on the road, not replying right away. Her words sound carefully chosen when she finally speaks. "What's your backup plan?"

Backup plan? She sees a flaw I'm missing in this one.

"What do you mean?"

"What if the rest don't let you worry about it later?"

I shake my head, not letting my mind go there. "That's something to worry about later, I guess."

Dylan doesn't say anything else, but I can tell it's bugging her.

The park is busy for October. There are plenty of people enjoying the decent weather and just as much traffic on the streets around the square. Dylan is lucky to find an open space right next to the park so that I don't have to cross the street when I get out.

She pulls in and reaches for the keys but I stop her. "You don't have to hang out here."

"I am not about to go on home, Elle." Dylan doesn't shut the SUV off, but her voice is firm.

"I'm fine, Dylan. Really. I don't want you wasting your day waiting around on me." I spot Milo walking toward us and gesture to him. "Besides, Milo is here. I won't be alone."

Dylan sees him and they wave at each other. She hesitates only a second more before saying, "Okay, but I'm not going home." I start to protest and she adds, "I won't sit here, either. I'll drive around, but that's as good as you're gonna get." This wasn't an easy decision for her.

"Thank you."

She brushes some hair behind my ear before lightly pushing my shoulder. "Now go on. Have fun. Text me if you need me."

"I will." I get out and close the door behind me, waving as I watch her leave.

I expect to see Milo next to me when I turn around, but he's still standing where he was a moment ago. He waves–that awkward way he does–and walks toward me. I meet him on the sidewalk between us.

The tension is obvious, but not like before, not like when we were sharing first kisses by the time sheets at work. It feels more... hesitant. Like we're unsure how to pick things back up

Even with the tension, though, Milo still seems excited to see me. He might not be letting it out like before, but he's never been very good at hiding it.

He gestures toward the path and we start walking, silently at first. Honestly, I didn't come prepared. I have no clue what to say.

Milo breaks the silence. "How are you?" It doesn't feel so loaded when it's him asking that question.

"I'm okay, I guess." I don't want to lie, but I don't want to ruin the date, either. "You?"

"Good. I'm good."

We fall silent again.

"Has the store been running okay?" I grasp for things to talk about, wishing our conversation would go as easy as it always has before.

"Yeah, Martha let me put up a Halloween Christmas tree in the front." He grins, some of the tension fading.

"Really?"

He nods, "Yeah. Rob wants to leave it up all year now and decorate it for every holiday." We both giggle at the idea.

There we are. There's that easy feeling.

"Are you still interested in me?" The words blurt out.

Milo stops, confusion on his face. "What?"

"I thought maybe since I pushed you away..." I struggle to find the right words, heat filling my cheeks.

Milo takes a step closer. "Of course I am." He shakes his head. "You've been through something that I cannot even imagine, Ellessy. Anyone would need space after that, and I've been trying to give it to you."

He's still interested. I haven't pushed him away.

Milo takes another step toward me, allowing a couple to squeeze past us on the sidewalk. He waits until they've passed before he says, "You can have as much space–as much time–as you need, Ellessy. I'm here. I'm not going anywhere."

I take a deep breath, staring at my feet as I say, "I'm trying to focus on the good things in my life, and right now you're the only good thing outside of Dylan." I look up at him and add, "You're the best good thing."

He stands there–eyes locked on mine–long enough for my anxiety to make itself known. I can't ignore it anymore.

He finally takes another step forward, leaving barely a foot of distance between us. "I can't tell you how much I want to pick things back up where we left off." His words come out slow and careful, but enveloped with his signature warmth. "And it's so good to see you out here trying to get back into the swing of things after everything you've been through."

I don't feel guilty for the smile he gives me this time. I should have focused on the good things all along.

"But..." My stomach drops as he says the word.

Anxiety comes into full focus, threatening to burst in my chest. "Do you still want to be with me?" My own words sound almost frantic as my breathing starts to pick up pace.

"Of course I do, Ellessy, I just don't think that's what you need right now."

I throw myself at him without even thinking, pulling him in and smashing my lips against his, begging for the spark we had the first time we kissed.

Milo's hands grasp my shoulders, but they push me away instead of pulling me in for more.

"Ellessy," He tries to catch his breath, his brows fraught with concern. "This is not like you." He shakes his head, his eyes searching mine.

I avoid his gaze, tears spilling over before I can stop them. "I thought you still wanted this…"

"I don't want to take advantage of you."

The bubble bursts.

I can't breathe. I can't think straight. Nothing is going the way it was supposed to.

Focusing on the good led me right to the kind of stuff I want to ignore.

Dylan was right.

What if the rest don't let you worry about it later?

I turn away and start walking, arguing with my thoughts as I go. Milo follows. He's saying something to me, but my mind feels squished in, like it's too narrow to process anything other than pain right now.

Why did I think I could ignore it? Why did I think this was the right plan? Or the right way to go about it?

Everything feels like it's spinning around me. I can't

catch my breath. All of the darkness I've been fighting to get away from pours back in. I keep walking–desperate–as if that might help me somehow run away from it all.

Who am I kidding? Nothing is going to change, and I don't want to be here.

I don't even know if I want to be alive.

Screams pierce the air as I'm violently tugged back, the roaring of my name nearly drowned out by the screeching of tires.

Milo is clutching me so tight, I can hear his heart beating. "You're okay. You're okay. You're okay." He keeps repeating the words.

I pull back enough to look around and try to figure out what happened. People are staring. A man is coming toward us from a car stopped in the road, a mixture of anger and concern crossing his face. Milo waves him away, saying, "She's okay. We're okay."

Tires screeching. Realization slams into me like the car that almost did.

I walked out into traffic.

Emotion takes over and my legs give out, Milo sinking to the ground with me. "You should've let me go." I fall apart in his arms, my body like a rag doll, tears streaming down my cheeks.

"Don't say that. You don't mean that." He puts his

hands on either side of my face and forces me to look into his eyes. "You can't say that."

I can see the pain across his face and feel worse for knowing I'm the reason it's there.

I cry harder. "It's not fair that I'm alive."

He moves his hands to my shoulders and jerks me away from the thought. "No. You can't say that, Ellessy. You can't." He brushes hair and tears from my face. "Because you're my best good thing, too."

The knife in my gut twists. How can I be his best good thing when– "I've been awful to you."

"You don't get to choose how hard grief hurts you."

He deserves so much better.

I shake my head. "I don't think I'll ever be me again. Things are never going to get back to normal."

I try to pull away, but he doesn't let go. "Look, I didn't know you before everything that happened to you. I don't know what your normal was. But I really enjoy getting to know the girl who likes poetry. Who loves sweet tea and skee-ball and was definitely named after a house fire." A tortured laugh breaks through my tears as Milo puts one hand on my cheek. "I really like you, Ellessy. *This* you."

I lean into his hand, holding it closer with both of mine. "Milo…"

"You don't have to say anything." He leans forward and kisses my forehead. "Just promise me that pulling you out of traffic isn't going to be a regular thing."

I don't want to lie to him. "I can't promise my mind won't go back there."

He shrugs. "Well, then I guess I'll be there to pull you back again."

Dylan comes running up to us, out of breath and frantic. "Is she okay? Are y'all okay? I couldn't get parked and tried and–"

"She's okay." Milo cuts through her worried ramble, standing and helping me to my own feet.

Dylan pulls me away from him, giving me a quick once-over before smashing me into a bear hug. "Don't you scare me like that again. You hear me? I don't ever wanna be scared like that over you again."

"I'm okay, Dylan." I struggle to get the words out with her squeezing me so tight. "I told you Milo would keep me safe."

She releases me and grabs Milo for a bear hug this time. "Thank God for you, kid." His face turns bright red.

"You scared me somethin' awful," Dylan says, turning back to me. "I mean it. I heard the tires screech and then I saw you and Milo on the ground. And when I couldn't find a place to park... I almost left it in the road."

I can feel the heat flushing my own face. "I'm sorry, Dylan."

"What was runnin' through your mind to make you do somethin' like that?"

I glance at Milo, but he doesn't say anything. "I, uh... I had the wrong plan." I swallow some of my pride and add, "The rest didn't wait until later."

Milo looks confused but Dylan nods. "I didn't think it would, kiddo." She lifts my chin so I'm looking at her. "Your mama didn't mean for you to ignore the bad things, Elle. She meant to make room for them. 'Cause bad things happen. Ain't nothin' you can do but learn to live with 'em.

"And you've got us here to keep you steady when the bad stuff catches up." Dylan slaps Milo on the back a little too hard like always, and adds, "Doesn't she?"

"She does." Milo's eyes catch mine. "We might need to look into one of those backpacks with the leash, though."

Dylan snorts. "I like you, kid."

One side of my mouth curls up. "I haven't completely pushed you away?"

He grins. "I'm not going anywhere unless you really want me to."

His words from earlier come to me again.

I didn't know you before everything that happened to you.

He's right. Milo didn't know me before my accident. He never got to meet the me I've been trying so hard to find again. Neither has Dylan, for that matter. The two most important people in my life now, and they're both here for the broken, grieving, anxiety-riddled mess I am now.

If they can accept me this way, why can't I?

I step toward him and hesitate only a moment before sliding my hand into his. "Do you want to go get lunch with us?"

Milo holds my hand a little firmer. "Sounds like a plan."

Twenty-Two

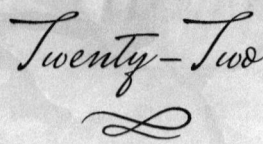

"Is he meeting us here or are we meeting him there?" Dylan tucks her phone in her pocket and grabs the keys.

I double check my messages. "He's meeting us there."

"And you're sure that's where you want to go?"

I smile. "That's where we always go to celebrate. It's tradition."

"I can't argue with tradition, can I?"

A text pops up on my phone. It's Milo. "He said he's already on his way there."

"I'd say that's our cue to scoot, then." She opens the door and gestures for me to lead the way.

We're meeting Milo at Goodwin's Steakhouse. I haven't been there in six months, not since the accident. I'm a little nervous to go back, especially on the roads in December, but I'm also excited for what we're celebrating.

It deserves the old tradition.

Dylan turns the radio up as one of her favorite songs comes on. "Sing it with me, kiddo!" I laugh and shake my head.

A weird sense of déjà vu hits me with a shiver down my spine. Dylan turns the music down long enough to ask, "Cold chill?" I nod and she turns it back up, turning the heat up with it.

Milo's truck is parked and running when we get there. He waves when he sees us.

"I swear that boy wouldn't be late if a snake bit him on the way and he hit the hospital first." Dylan chuckles.

We park and get out, meeting Milo on the way to the entrance. Dylan pulls him in for a hug and a slap on the back. He grins, no doubt expecting it at this point.

He grabs my hand and leans down for a quick kiss before we head inside and away from the cold.

"Dang it, I didn't even think to call ahead for a reservation," Dylan says, looking around at the people already waiting.

"Milo called." My voice is almost sing-song.

He smiles and steps up to give his name to the woman at the podium. "Milo Fellows." She tells us they're clearing a table now and it will be ready in a few moments.

"Lucky you two were on it," Dylan says.

"We always are." Milo winks and squeezes my hand.

"Ugh, you two are so adorable, it's disgustin'." Dylan chuckles, and I know I'm the one to blush this time.

Another hostess takes us to back of the restaurant. "I hope a booth is okay," she says, setting out menus as we slide in, Dylan on one side and Milo next to me.

"This is fine, thank you." I smile at her, idly wondering if she was here that night. Or what about the waiter who just joined us? Was he here?

I let the thought fade as he asks, "Can I get drink orders for you guys?"

Milo and I both order sweet tea.

"Better make it three, and keep 'em comin'," Dylan says.

"Three sweet teas it is." He leaves us to look over our menus.

"Shoo, everything here looks good to me." Dylan lifts her menu closer to–and then away from–her face. She must have forgotten her reading glasses at home.

"I agree," Milo says, wrapping his arm around my shoulder and scooting me closer.

"I'm going to try this." I point to the pot pie on his menu.

"I think I'll try it, too." He grins and moves our menus to the edge of the table.

"What are you two plannin' to try?"

"The pot pie." Milo points at it.

Dylan frowns. "I think I'll just take a steak and call it a day."

Our waiter returns a moment later with our drinks and leaves with our orders.

Milo picks up his glass, raising it in front of us. "A toast?"

I lift my own drink. "To Milo officially getting his Associate's Degree and being one step closer to becoming an Occupational Therapist."

He blushes and says, "I still have more schooling to go... How about, to Lowercase accepting her promotion to manager at the store?"

Dylan raises her glass and clinks it against ours. "I can drink to both of those."

We clink glasses one more time and all drink.

"So, does this mean for sure that you're not doin' college?" Dylan asks.

We talked a lot after Rob offered me the position

about whether or not I wanted to go to college. Oakvale never rescinded their offer, but it doesn't feel right to go without Lilah–even if I know she'd tell me that's not a reason to turn it down. We also talked about the idea of going to Kassemme Community College where Milo just graduated, even if only for a few classes.

I just don't know what I want to do anymore–wouldn't even know what to major in. That's a lot of money to drop on something I'm not sure about, and scholarships aren't a guarantee.

"Not for now, anyway." Part of me feels like I'm letting Mom and Lilah down, but I also know they'd want me to do what's best for me. And I think this is it. "I'm excited I get to be a manager and help Rob and Martha with the shop."

"You should be." Milo says. "You get to pick who replaces me when I'm off helping people get better." He puffs out his chest and looks up like he's posing for a comic book cover.

"We've still got a few years before that, Trip."

"Aw..." He deflates at that nickname. I smile and kiss his cheek.

"I really am proud of you, kiddo," Dylan says, bringing something serious back to the moment. "After everything you've been through, it's good to see you takin' this head on and being excited about somethin'."

I can feel the heat in my cheeks again. "I'm nervous about the responsibility and my anxiety–"

"Don't be." Dylan waves it away. "You'll be fine and then some."

"You know the store just as well as Rob and Martha do. You're gonna be awesome." Milo pulls me in and kisses my forehead.

"Yeah, you're gonna do fine, kiddo. You got this. And you've got Milo and Abbie and Martha and Rob there for the times you don't." She counts them off on her fingers.

"I still feel bad that Abbie didn't get the offer."

Dylan waves my words away. "You know she didn't want it and Rob knew she didn't want it. She told you as much when she said they were planning to offer it to you."

"You deserve this promotion, Lowercase." Milo pauses and adds, "I might have to start calling you 'Capital' now that you're working the big kid job."

I roll my eyes. "I guess that's better than 'House Fire'."

"Seriously, though, you deserve the job and you're going to do fine."

"And you know everyone there will help you when

your anxiety gets to actin' hateful." Dylan slaps her hand down on the table. "Hell, I'll come in there and help if I have to."

I laugh. "You're right. Both of you."

"Damn right we are." She winks at me as she lifts her glass and takes a drink.

Dylan is a big part of the reason I took the job. I was worried that my anxiety would be too big of a hurdle with taking on a management position, that my fears about what might go wrong would get in the way. But she encouraged me to take the risk, anyway. "I'll help you with the rest of it," she said. I know I'm not going into this alone.

"So what comes next, kiddo? What's the plan?"

It doesn't escape me that the last time I was here, Lilah and I sat across from Mom as she asked me the same thing.

"Uh... This right here." I take a deep breath and smile. "Dinner with my favorite people, and then a movie with my boyfriend after." I squeeze Milo's hand and he pulls me in for another kiss. I never get tired of those and I'm sure he knows it.

"Does this mean we're done with plans?" Dylan asks.

"No." I shake my head. "I'm just leaving a little more wiggle room."

Milo pulls over the dessert menu. "Speaking of wiggle room, are we leaving some for dessert before we go to the movies?"

"Just let me know when you're ready for it," our waiter says, sliding over with our food just in time to catch Milo's comment.

Dylan cuts a piece from her steak, dipping it in the mashed potatoes before she shoves it in her mouth. "If we're judgin' this place by the way they cook a steak, they get five stars from me."

I try a bite of the pot pie I ordered, waiting for Milo to try his before I say anything.

"I'm glad I went with your choice. This is good." He grins. "What do you think?"

"I like it." I smile and keep eating, thankful I decided to be spontaneous and try something new this time.

"What movie are y'all going to see?"

"That one romantic comedy that just came out, " I say.

"The Christmas one?" Milo nods and Dylan adds, "How'd she rope you into that mess?"

I grin. "Milo picked it out."

Dylan laughs and Milo defends his choice. "Christmas movies are my favorite, thank you."

"I shoulda known." Dylan chuckles and slices off

another piece of her steak. "I'll find us some *good* movies to watch this weekend, kiddo." She winks at me, stuffing the bite into her mouth. "Somethin' with a different kind of action."

"Do I get to watch these 'good movies' this weekend?" Milo makes air quotes as he says it.

"Of course! You're bringin' the pizza."

"Oh, I'm there to supply food?" Milo fakes offence.

"Don't worry, we'll make dessert," I assure him.

Dylan arches a brow. "We will?"

"Mom's brownies are next." Dylan and I have been working through Mom's recipe book.

"I guess we're making brownies, then."

"I think I can bring pizza if I'm getting brownies."

"Like you would need a reason to bring pizza in the first place, kid." Dylan laughs. "That's like saying Elle needs a reason to stop for a sweet tea."

Milo gives Dylan a look as he pushes his plate to the side. "Do you hear this, Lowercase?"

"I do, and she's not wrong." I shrug.

Milo scoffs and pulls the dessert menu back over. "So are we getting dessert before the movie?" He glances at his phone. "We have time."

"I suppose you could share one of those with me." I point to the lava cake. Milo looks around for our waiter.

"Are you going to get any dessert, Dylan?" I ask as she pushes her plate to the side.

"Nah." She pulls her wallet out and sets enough cash to cover everything and then some on the table. "I think I'll get on outta here and leave you kids to it."

"See you at home?"

"See you at home, kiddo." She scoots out of the booth and stands. "Y'all text me when you get there. And when you're on your way back, too."

"We will. Thanks for lunch, Dylan."

She pats him on the back. "Congrats on your degree, Milo."

"And Ellessy's promotion." He grins and nudges me.

"That too." Dylan smiles. "Have fun, you two." She walks away, her booming voice startling the family in the booth next to us as she hollers back, "Don't forget to text me!"

Our waiter takes that as his cue to come over and clear our plates, promising to return with our dessert order soon.

Milo moves around to sit across from me. "Congratulations, Ellessy Jane 'House Fire' 'Lowercase' Porter." He lifts his drink.

"Congratulations, Milo Oliver 'Trip' Fellows." I raise my glass to meet his.

We both grin like a couple of smitten kids and clink our glasses.

Maybe the old normal was better. Maybe it was just different. But if I have to accept a new one, I'd say this is the right one to have.

Acknowledgments

Special thanks to everyone who helped me make this dream a reality.

All the people who pushed me every step of the way and kept reminding me that they wanted to read my books someday.

My husband, Ryan, who is my best friend, great love, and number one supporter in everything I set my mind to.

My close friend and alpha reader, Abbie, who is the reason I've been able to finally finish any of my writing projects and get to the point of publishing.

My cover artist, Ali, who is amazing to work with and such a kind, compassionate, and talented person that I'm happy to also call a friend.

All of my family and friends, too many to name, who have always been there and encouraged me along the way.

(I will name my nieces, though. Annie, Jamie, and Lacie. Thanks for always believing in Aunt Hayley.)

My late mother, who always made me believe I could make my dream come true.

My late best friend, Shanna, who was my very first number one fan and inspiration.

My late friend, Lina, who shared my passion for books and always encouraged my writing.

All of the teachers from my childhood and college days who nurtured my dream and helped me build it.

All of the writing groups I've joined and mostly talk about things other than writing in.

Those that follow me on Patreon.

And anyone else who has followed me on my journey or helped me along the way.

Thank you.

About the Author

Hayley B Halliwell is a queer author living in southern Missouri with her husband of over a decade, and their cat, Roswell Soup. When she isn't writing or working her day job, she can usually be found crocheting or playing video games. She is aware of the contrast between those two. Hayley is very open about living with mental illness and chronic pain, and hopes to break the stigma surrounding them.

- threads.net/@hayleybhalliwell
- facebook.com/hayleybhalliwell
- instagram.com/hayleybhalliwell
- patreon.com/HayleyBHaliwell
- tiktok.com/@TikTok.com@hayleybhalliwell

About the Cover Artist

Ali is an artist and illustrator based in the U.S., where she lives with her husband and children. She loves to create cozy illustrations that inspire hope and celebrate the simple joys of everyday life. Ali draws inspiration from nature, animals, vintage fashion, books, and her kids. When she's not creating art, she enjoys spending time with her family, reading, knitting, sewing, baking, and playing cozy games. You can find her art on Instagram and Threads, where she shares under the name @juniper.charm.

instagram.com/juniper.charm
threads.net/@juniper.charm

Also by Hayley B Halliwell

THE FOLLOWING POETRY COLLECTIONS

Garden Your Soul

Flavors of Weird

Picket Fence Signs

www.ingramcontent.com/pod-product-compliance
Lightning Source LLC
LaVergne TN
LVHW041749060526
838201LV00046B/953